10 SHORT STORIES

YOU **MUST** READ

THIS YEAR

10 SHORT STORIES
YOU **MUST** READ
THIS YEAR

Robert Drewe

Anita Heiss

Toni Jordan

Tom Keneally

Kathy Lette

Monica McInerney

William McInnes

Melina Marchetta

Jack Marx

Peter Temple

Books Alive is an Australian Government initiative developed through the Australia Council for the Arts, the Australian Government's arts funding and advisory body.

BOOKS ALIVE 2009

10 SHORT STORIES YOU MUST READ THIS YEAR

First published in Australia in 2009 by
The Australia Council
www.australiacouncil.gov.au

National Library of Australia Cataloguing-in-Publication entry

Title: 10 short stories you must read this year.
ISBN: 9780731814329 (pbk.)
Subjects: Short stories, Australian.
Dewey Number: A823.0108

Cover design by Cave Design
Typeset by Midland Typesetters

Printed in Australia by Griffin Press

The paper used to produce this book is a natural, recyclable product made from wood
grown in sustainable plantation forests. The manufacturing processes conform to the
environmental regulations in the country of origin.

10 9 8 7 6 5 4 3 2 1

Foreword

I have to thank my grandmother for sparking my passion for reading. When I was ten she gave me my first Charles Dickens novel, and from then on, every Christmas and birthday she gave me another one. By the time I was twenty I'd read all of Dickens and was hooked on reading for life.

So as an avid reader and book lover I'm thrilled to welcome you to this dazzling collection of stories written by some of our best writers exclusively for the 2009 Books Alive campaign. It's yours free when you buy one of the fifty books listed in the Guide to 50 Books You Can't Put Down during the campaign period, which this year is 26 August to 30 September.

Whether you like humour, chick lit, or just a great read whatever the genre, you'll find something in here to enjoy. Such as Robert Drewe's brilliantly observed wry and witty story about two old friends in love with the same woman. Or Monica McInerney's warmly touching story of Elizabeth, who writes Christmas letters to rival the best novels. Or Booker Prize winner Tom Keneally's moving tale of a country schoolteacher and a young Sudanese student. And Jack Marx's fresh and blackly funny 'letter' from a drunken old man to his long-gone wife.

Now in its eighth year, Books Alive is an initiative generously supported by the Australian Government. It's the largest annual promotion of books and reading in Australia, and its aim is simple: to encourage all of us to put up our feet, switch off our screens and get reading. With this wonderful collection of stories, we can all take a little time out to do just that.

So if you haven't already, pick up a copy of the Guide to 50 Books You Can't Put Down. Buy one of the fifty books and receive your free book. And get reading!

Sandra Yates AO
Chair – Books Alive
Sydney
August 2009

Contents

1

A View of Mount Warning

Robert Drewe

Ever since Miss Burridge's Infants' class at Alstonville Public, Russell Garrett and Max Hodder had been close friends. They'd made speeches at each other's 21st birthday party and as best man at one another's weddings, Russell doing the honours at both Max's marriages, the big Anglican ceremony at St Mark's and the celebrant's all-white, natural-fibres affair held at low tide between Tibetan prayer flags on the sands of Cape Byron.

Now, over New Year's Day pre-lunch beers, while the meat sizzled on the Beef King and Max's wife Sophie prepared the salad indoors, Russell winced at the knowledge that this year they would both turn fifty. So they'd known each other forty-five years. 'Food for thought, eh?' he said, as they allowed the shiraz to breathe.

Other than those forty-five years, however, Russell and Max didn't really have much in common nowadays. Yes, there had been crucial episodes where their bond had been tight: the icy August morning when Max had dragged the heavier Russell, concussed by a stranger's runaway surfboard, first to the surface and then ashore; and of course Russell's regular physical backup to Max's teenage braggadocio. But now they were friends simply because they'd always been friends. They'd stayed in touch despite their lives taking different paths, maybe *because* their lives had taken different paths – and because they lived nine hundred kilometres apart and only saw each other three or four times annually, including every New Year at the Hodders' house.

Since their north-coast surfing adolescence Max Hodder had dropped out of engineering at UNSW, married his high-school girlfriend, leapt into Northern Rivers real estate, made a pile in the sea-change boom of the '90s, divorced and remarried, and retired early to Byron Bay, to a three-storey Watego's Beach cliff-house, a vertical engineering feat poised dramatically above the humpback whales' migration route.

Over recent visits Russell had perceived a gradual change in his friend. The wit and imagination Max had shown in snapping up both the striking Sophie Howson and that prized white-water view – of the same exposed point break and north-east swells they'd surfed endlessly at sixteen – were no longer evident.

Drastically, in Russell's mind (he still kept his old boards ready for action in the Hodders' garage), Max seemed to have wearied of surfing. In his premature retirement, having attained the woman and house he wanted,

Max appeared to be letting life pass him by. He was taking it easy. Comfortably and purposefully ageing, he spent his days in his shuttered study, forgoing the vista, the beach, the health-giving ocean for his wine cellar and cable television's endless spool of sports.

Russell Garrett, on the other hand, living and working far from the ocean, was running the same old race year after year. He'd emerged from veterinary science at Queensland Uni to take over an old-established horse practice at Rock Forest, outside Bathurst in the central west. Eschewing sick cats, dogs and canaries for horses meant worse hours and considerable travel and inconvenience (horses had a habit of falling ill on public holidays), and he couldn't afford to retire. Garrett Equine Services had seen both ends of thousands of those surprisingly frail, nervy and accident-prone creatures, with no doubt hundreds more extremities to come, and lately Russell's life was the most exhausting it had ever been. His marriage had broken up twelve months before, at the start of the equine flu epidemic. Even without the emotional upheaval it had been a rough year for a country vet.

So while the atmosphere at the home of his long-time friend was initially more awkward without Estelle present, and with Max oddly engrossed in TV sports round-ups, Russell's first two beers of the year didn't touch the sides. New Year's Eve had been taxing, unexpected and, finally, sleepless. But January 1 was supposed to be a day of optimism. Although slightly rusty in the joints, he'd already hit the beach and the early-morning swells curling past the cape. The surf had worked its old magic and he was on holidays in familiar company on the coast he loved. The dead year was over and done with, and now lunch was fragrantly grilling on the barbecue.

Reclining in a deckchair on the Hodders' terrace, Russell was surrendering to the sunny breeze and the sweeping panorama of the bay and the Nightcap Range. For the first time ever he was searching for another conversational opening when Max, lowering his voice as he flipped the steaks, murmured, 'I had enough of those bloody spam emails pestering me. So I gave Viagra a whirl.'

'Really?' Russell felt his left eyelid twitch. When it kept fluttering he turned his attention to the view. As always, his eyes sought out the tallest peak, rising through the mauve clouds today like a holy Shangri-La mountain. Mount Warning, named by Captain Cook as he sailed north on the *Endeavour* in 1770, and steeped in Aboriginal spirituality for many millennia before that. How many school projects had he prepared on Mount Warning? How many mountain ranges had he built out of egg cartons?

His eyelid still fluttered involuntarily. Understandably in the circumstances, his nerves could still take him by surprise. For at least ten years, in fact ever since the day of their marriage, he'd been in love with his oldest friend's wife.

'Well, it definitely works. I was like a bloody eighteen-year-old again.'

'Good for you.' Russell didn't want to hear this. He could bear the idea of Sophie and Max Hodder's physical relationship only if it was conducted as he observed it: vertical and fully clothed. His was a melancholy and insurmountable jealousy, compounded by guilt. Of course his feelings for Sophie were unrequited, but even if she'd been aware of them and magically, enthusiastically, reciprocated, she was the wife of his boyhood friend – Max's second and twelve-years-younger wife – and therefore out of bounds, now and forever.

Such was the nature of his infatuation, however, that even as he tussled with guilt one moment, deliberately avoiding her presence, the next minute he'd be torturing himself with the smallest hints and snatched glances. She'd bustle and bend and flip her hair from her forehead and he'd have to tear his eyes from the thrilling sight of her rinsing dishes at the kitchen sink, arranging flowers, making coffee. This woman's actions were never mundane.

It was obvious she liked talking to him, and often seemed to sparkle in his company. She must have noticed that at any party, after several drinks, he self-consciously drifted to her side. Indeed, she often blithely joined him, too. Sometimes she even flirted with him, and his blood pounded with the excitement of possibilities. But then she'd cheerily turn elsewhere, and behave the same way with Max's other friends, and he'd feel like a sulking fifteen-year-old. Sophie was a friendly person.

In saner moments back in the Bathurst district, bouncing along a gravel road on his way to deal with some Shetland's or Arab's hoof thrush or rain scald, or an old thoroughbred's well-earned arthritis, he reasoned that her public squeeze of his arm, the chest prod or cheek pat, could merely be her tactile nature. Or was she subtly testing him? Was Sophie a tease? No, she was a decent, straightforward person. But at night before sleep he was at his least realistic. How could he not dwell on the *perhaps* and the *maybe* and the delicious *what if*? As he had last night, of all nights.

Whenever he saw her she had him in a flurry of confusion. In her presence, aching for her trailing hostessy fingers, the accidentally brushed knees, the casual touch, he always felt like a teenager. As she passed by his chair he'd clench his stomach muscles and surreptitiously flex his biceps. Willing her, *touch me.* Then he felt like a fool.

As time passed and Russell tossed these conflicting daydreams back and forth after every get-together, he still managed to keep his feelings hidden. He was doomed to silently adore everything about her, from her generous spirit and quick humour to that slightly crooked front tooth and occasionally lazy left eyelid. Of course he noticed these small flaws; every imperfection was a sensual asset.

It wasn't just sex, he convinced himself. He genuinely admired her. While he envied her loyalty to her husband, he also respected it; the way she dutifully waited on Max with drinks and food. Sophie *attended* to him. The thing was, he, Russell, also *liked* her – and of course phlegmatic Hodder, entrenched in front of Fox Sports all day watching lacrosse and snooker and Japanese rugby, a mid-morning jug of Bloody Marys by his elbow, a sequence of afternoon and evening wine bottles, didn't deserve or appreciate her at all.

When Russell thought about it, not since the moment he fell for her, at their windy wedding on the cape, with the northerly whipping the Tibetan prayer flags and exposing the laughing bride's thighs, had he seen Max embrace her. On Sophie's behalf, Russell was offended. And gladdened. It was bewildering how Max could treat her so neglectfully when he, Russell, was so overwhelmed by her creamy limbs and cleavage and careless fair hair – the whole sexual package – that he fell into a brief catatonic state whenever they hugged hello and goodbye.

While he dwelt regularly on the look and feel of Sophie, recalling the lively pressure of her body in those jolly public embraces, as time passed after each contact he'd momentarily come to his senses. He'd be standing in some urinous country stable or faecal paddock, shin-deep in mud and cowpats, crows gagging overhead and the whiff of something decomposing nearby, and he'd say it aloud: 'It's a dream.'

It would never come to anything. If his marriage to Estelle wasn't exactly a living heaven, there was a bond there, and two grown children, and a long rapport that he wasn't willing to deny. Stamping back to the Land Cruiser, full of sad determination, he'd once again place the possibility of a romance with Sophie in fantasy territory, in the bittersweet category of never-to-be. A sweetly carnal version of winning Lotto.

Then, quite abruptly, these overlapping quandaries produced some new dilemmas to both confuse him and rekindle his hopes. The first, a surprise to him, if not to Estelle, was that their marriage of twenty-four years suddenly disintegrated. (Nothing to do with his longing for a fantasy woman whom he'd never even kissed, he told himself.) It was Estelle who pulled the plug on him, and Daniel and Lily, in order to embark on the 'personal journey' she'd apparently promised herself before she turned fifty, and as soon as the children reached twenty-one. She also made it clear that her journey was not a trip that stopped at his station.

Maritally jettisoned, he would have been more devastated if it hadn't been for the equine epidemic. Oddly, the horse flu got him through; he was so overworked he didn't have the time to languish. And eventually, as the disease finally ebbed, it dawned on him that he was single again, no longer required to be a dutiful and faithful husband – maybe there was a bright side to this – and in the usual dank three a.m. cave of despair there appeared a chink of light. He'd soon be seeing Sophie again.

Now, on this first day of the new year, as the piquant smoke of beef marinade drifted across the terrace and out to sea, here was Max waving barbecue tongs and muttering, 'I did my Viagra research up at the Gold Coast. At good old Madame Peaches.' Almost simultaneously, two electric flashes struck Russell. *So, not with Sophie.* And then, *Max visits prostitutes.*

Russell made the appropriate responses, the whistle, the raised eyebrow, but his beer suddenly tasted metallic – flat, warm, like sucking cutlery – and he poured himself a shiraz. My God, Max was winking at him. Max was grinning. Max did a little disco jig so his chest fat jiggled in his T-shirt, and he snapped the barbecue tongs over his head as if they were crab nippers or castanets. His oldest friend had turned into a sly, lazy, alcoholic shithead.

He kept his voice flat. 'You go there often?' Meaning brothels. Five or six times a year, he gathered. Max and three cronies disappeared on rollicking all-boys sporting holidays to Brisbane, Sydney, Melbourne, the Gold Coast. To Test matches, football finals, race meetings, fishing trips – and brothels. Much avid organising was involved. The Veterans' Sporting Club, they called themselves. The VSC.

'You're now in the company of the president of the VSC,' Max announced. He'd come to life all of a sudden.

The sunlight brought out his new high colour, the pouchy eyes and broken veins. Russell thought he saw a hint of jaundice in the eyes, but Max's eyes wouldn't meet his. Max snippety-snapped the meat tongs again and attempted more weak humour. 'Order, order! The meeting will come to order!' This was a rare garrulous burst. It was like being ear-bashed by a drunken stranger in a pub.

Russell recognised something of powerful and limitless potential here, also something that would never occur. Despite its possible rewards – their marriage instantly ending, Sophie flying into his sympathetic arms – the idea of him spilling the beans, or even indirectly allowing the beans to be spilt, was beyond the pale. The Old Mates Rule. Max knew that. He knew that. It went without saying. And if he did do so, Sophie would despise the messenger. And he would despise himself.

Russell hated Max at that moment. Even with a mouthful of wine, he still tasted knives and forks on his tongue.

Max gave the barbecue a moment's attention, put down the tongs and yelled out to Sophie, 'Steak's ready!' Then to Russell he said, 'Thanks again for last night, by the way. Missing the party and all.'

Russell breathed in some sea air. 'That's fine.' For him, much of New Year's Eve had passed in a reeking stall in the stable of Max's hinterland property at Clunes. Not that he regretted it at all. Here Sophie Hodder kept her four horses – three geldings and a 22-year-old bay mare. In the late afternoon the mare had lain down, writhing and kicking and snapping at the dirt, and refused to stand. No local vets were available on this major party evening and Sophie had phoned him in tears. The horse was in a bad way. It was seven o'clock by then, and he was still an hour south on the Pacific Highway. He hadn't even begun his holiday. 'I'll meet you there,' he said.

She was wide-eyed and agitated when he arrived. Western-clad, kneeling by the horizontal mare, jumping up, pacing and waving her arms, she came across like a feisty rancher's daughter in a movie. He was always deliberately calm and calming on the job, to people and to animals. He patted her shoulder. 'I remember seeing you try out this old girl,' he said.

Seven or eight years ago he'd been there at her request to check out the mare's condition; she was thinking of buying her. He'd watched them walking the riding arena, the clearest memory. The metronomic gait of the horse, and Sophie's body flowing into the rising trot. Blonde hair swinging below her helmet, strands gathered in a child's ponytail. The jounce of her breasts increasing in the canter; the rise and fall of her tightly jodhpured seat. The hypnotic sexual tempo of her ups and downs.

'So, should I buy her?' she asked him.

He even recalled the pale-blue polo shirt, her exercise-blush from cheek to neck, and the frown of concentration that completed her intensely female look. Her vividness made him feel countrified and khaki-coloured by comparison. He could have eaten her up, boots and all. 'You look good together,' he said.

Max had remained in the car throughout, reading the paper like a bored father.

This time she was in grass-stained jeans, from kneeling. 'Help me get her on her feet,' he said. 'Let's walk her.' In the fig trees around the paddock, squealing fruit bats were rousing themselves and flapping heavily over their heads. The patient had colic. 'Horses are drama queens,' he said.

By ten-thirty he'd led the mare into the stable stall and with mineral oil and a stomach tube induced her to defecate freely, whereupon she snorted, stamped, tossed her head, and soon recovered. He was still holding the mare's head-collar and both of them were shit-soiled when Sophie leant in and kissed him. She had straw in her hair. Just a quick kiss of gratitude, but firmly on the lips.

In those first hours of the new year, even after the long drive to Watego's and several drinks, Russell found it hard to sleep. All along the coast, snatches of laughter and party music carried on the breeze. Eventually the voices and music faded, and doors slammed, and cars drove away. Once, his body jumped to footsteps on the stairs. At first light he would get his old Malibu from the garage and hit the water. But until dawn he lay alert, listening to the mixed rhythm of the surf and Max's proprietorial snores rumbling from the master bedroom.

• •

The Hodders served a simple New Year's lunch on the terrace. Steak, Moroccan salad, local fruits – tamarillos, guavas, papayas, mangoes – and cheeses to suit the wines. Summery Australia stretched ahead like a double-page spread in a travel magazine. The south-easterly tempered the heat of the sun, and in the small waves off the cape schools of surfers and dolphins gently surged and mingled. Like the Paramount Pictures trademark, or the volcano it had once been, Mount Warning rose dramatically from the lavender clouds over the range.

Competitively sited on the edge of the terrace so he wouldn't miss a ball or a single run, Max's widescreen TV displayed the murmuring green vista of Test cricket. Russell wondered if Max was using the cricket to avoid conversation. This was ridiculous. After lunch he said to his old surf companion, 'The wind's changed. Get your board. They're pumping.'

'Maybe later,' said Max.

By mid-afternoon the breeze had dropped altogether and Russell and Sophie strolled down to the beach for a swim. Max declined in favour of the cricket and a chilled bottle of pinot. And so passed the first day of the new year.

As night fell, Max was dozing in his study in front of a Korea–Estonia soccer match. Their swimming costumes long since dried on their bodies, Russell and Sophie were drinking on the terrace, and in no hurry to end the evening.

To avoid the moths and Christmas beetles, Sophie turned off the terrace lights and they sat in the shadows. To Russell, in a rare daze of fatigue, confidence and good humour, this was surprisingly thrilling, reminiscent of childhood Murder in the Dark and Spin the Bottle. In this pleasant state he discovered that without any conscious effort they were sitting confidentially together, their knees and foreheads almost brushing.

Somehow their bare knees soon did connect, and remained firmly pressed together. The warmth this engendered seemed important and correct for such a pair of rapidly conjoining souls. Neither their intent expressions nor their conversation changed when he put his hands on Sophie's cool upper arms and squeezed them for a few seconds. Though the smallest alarm bell sounded with the touch of her smooth biceps, it was stilled by a blood-tingling new sensation, like the continuation of an actual dream: a glorious lack of restraint.

Below them the tide sparkled like soda. 'I'm allowed to be drunk,' Russell said, looking down at the beach. 'Firstly, I'm on holidays. Secondly, I'm going nowhere. And thirdly, I'm watching stingrays hunting in the moonlight.'

It was true. In the moonlit shallows, a school of rays, working gracefully in unison, was rounding up silver pilchards. The rays were ushering the tiny swarming fish into shore, enveloping and cornering them, and in their skittering panic the pilchards trailed strings of phosphorescence.

'Is this happening?' he asked Sophie, as much about the change in circumstances as the glistening hunt below. 'Or am I imagining it?'

'I think something's happening,' she said.

Their foreheads were also brushing now. Although it may have been melodramatic and dated of him to ask so solemnly, 'Can we kiss now?', after ten years of infatuation and frustration it seemed chivalrous and fitting. So he did, and there was no hesitation from Sophie. Still sitting, bare knees pressing against bare knees, they held each other and kissed for a long moment.

The sensation of kissing her seemed so unique that new words were needed for the open, moist warmth of her mouth, her lips' softness, the willingness of her embrace. When they eventually drew apart, it was with shock at themselves and the world's sudden echoing silence.

The television was off in the study and the stillness was abruptly broken by the clattering rumble of the refrigerator's ice server. It thundered like an avalanche. Ice cubes tumbled endlessly into what must have been the world's deepest glass. Finally the rumbling stopped. The door from the terrace to the kitchen was open and Max was standing by the refrigerator, wearing only purple boxer shorts in a dice pattern and staring out into the night.

• •

Russell lay in the spare bedroom recalling the rapture of the kiss on the terrace – he still couldn't believe it had actually happened – and the shock of being illicit lovers caught out. His pulse pounding in his ears, he relived the kiss over and over again. He felt both marvellously elated and nauseous with disloyalty. What had happened to his principles?

But had the kiss really been spotted? Perhaps the timing had just favoured them by a second or two. Maybe it had been too dark anyway. Did Max see them, and then purposely make that din with the ice cubes? Or, dulled by booze and sleep, had he blearily padded into the kitchen, filled his glass with ice, then randomly gazed out to sea?

Fortunately they'd been too stunned to panic. In any case it would have been crazy to jump up guiltily from the embrace. So, desperately hopeful of that one or two extra seconds, they'd remained where they were, slanting marginally away from each other now, giving the impression of being a couple merely engrossed in conversation.

To a witness it would clearly appear a serious tete-a-tete, maybe questionably familiar, but less intimate than being caught kissing the onlooker's wife.

Russell could almost convince himself there was nothing to worry about. Max had stood there, his stomach overlapping his dice-patterned boxers, filled a glass with ice, uttered nothing, and exited the room. So after a short interval, as if at a given signal, he and Sophie emphatically scraped back their chairs, moved around busily, chatting loudly while clearing plates and carrying glasses to the kitchen sink.

They stood at the sink, rinsing their wine glasses and looking obliquely at each other. He saw Sophie's cheeks blooming with the same flush as when she cantered her mare that day in the arena, while he felt sixteen again, hollowed out by excitement and tension, and perilously in love. He glanced around, wily as a spy, and stepped forward to risk another kiss. She raised her eyebrows at his nerve, patted at his chest and quickly pecked his lips. Shortly afterwards, calling 'Goodnight, goodnight!' they went upstairs to their separate bedrooms and he lay on top of his bedspread, still in his board shorts, his head swimming.

The next sound to register was kookaburras at dawn, and when he struggled to the toilet, headachy and half-asleep, the reflection of the sun was a golden radiance filling the bathroom mirror. Immediately he remembered the kiss and its aftermath, and was euphoric and anxious all over again.

It surprised him to see he was still wearing board shorts from the day before. Convenient, though; he needed to hit the surf immediately to clear his head and provide a breathing space for the events to follow. Time to think things out.

But her kiss still filled his mind. From the bathroom window the sky was red over the cape and strings of parrot-coloured cloud streamed across the horizon. A sullen swell was rolling ashore and the dawn seemed charged with pre-storm electricity. The thought of her lying mere metres away, warm and sleeping, and the incontrovertible fact of their liaison, made him catch his breath.

On his way downstairs he heard the TV going in Max's study. The sound made him even edgier. But sooner or later he had to face him. He forced himself to look into the room. Max was slumped in his armchair, a succession of neck, chest and belly rolls flowing down his torso, a kimono hanging open over his boxer shorts, sipping a tomato-looking drink.

'Morning, Maxie,' Russell said. Was it his guilt that put him on the front foot now, made him sound so disapproving? 'Six o'clock. You've put the boat out early.'

'Good morning. And it's juice.' Max's hairless, bone-white legs were up on the coffee table. Yesterday's cricket highlights flashed past on-screen, each highlight – a six over the fence, a shattered wicket, a difficult catch – greeted by a mysteriously loud crowd reaction from spectators' stands that appeared almost empty. Max drained the glass and looked up. His red, puffy eyes could be blamed on excessive alcohol. Or, the thought abruptly shocked Russell, on recent weeping.

'I suppose a surf is out of the question? Do us both good,' Russell said.

'Not today.'

Russell felt so uneasy he had to ask. 'Are you okay, old man?'

'Hunky-dory, old fruit.' Still half-gazing at the TV, Max reached into a kimono pocket and withdrew a small packet. 'Industrial strength, recommended by this Chinese quack up the coast. I've been looking forward to trying them out. I took two – they should be working pretty well by the time she wakes up.' He made the universal fist and stiff forearm.

Russell's eyelid began vigorously fluttering.

'Trouble is, when they dilate your blood vessels they make your eyes bloody red.'

Russell's eye-flutter proceeded apace.

Max turned towards him now. 'I've got the Veuve in the ice bucket. I usually do some smoked salmon. Caviar. Hard-boiled egg. Little toasty fingers. I go to a bit of trouble for our weekly extravaganza. Sophie likes a long decadent breakfast beforehand.'

Russell began heading out the door. A tin-coloured sea loomed all around and the mountains were indiscernible in the clouds.

Max called after him, raising his voice over the television. 'Listen, could you do us a favour and stay out there in the water for a couple of hours?'

2

Hate at First Sight

Kathy Lette

'What do you *mean* you're moving to the outback?' Louise's words were lost in her sister's slipstream, as Jane barrelled down the stone steps to stash another box in the boot of her battered Mustang. '*Why?*'

'The man shortage,' Jane grunted glumly. 'All the men in Sydney are married or gay.' She pushed back up the stairs past her immaculately groomed older sister to fetch more possessions from the landing outside her flat. 'Or married *and* gay.'

Louise tottered in vertiginous heels towards her sister's car, which was parked precariously halfway up on the curb. The uneven pavement of inner-city Redfern made her feel as though she were a toddler taking to the ice. 'Weren't you even going to tell me?'

'Why bother? I knew you'd just try to talk me out of it,' Jane replied fractiously, strapping her cello case into the back seat. It was typical of Jane to take up the cello as a child when a clarinet or a flute would have been so much more convenient.

'Oh well, that's just lovely, isn't it? Thank God I happened to drop in on the way home from court. My case settled, by the way. Thanks for asking.'

'I thought of writing to you, Louise, but what could I say? "So glad your life's perfect – engaged to legal eagle, great job, mortgage as small as your waist, Designer Genes inherited from mum and dad . . . but I'm buggering off because I'm thirty-two and my eggs are rotting in my ovaries." But there just didn't seem to be a Hallmark card to cover that,' she deadpanned.

Though only separated by thirteen months, Louise and Jane were not the type of sisters to sit around exchanging pleasantries about the asparagus. They'd spent their youth using each other as dartboards. Basically they had the same rapport as a gun-toting Islamic fundamentalist and the winner of this year's 'Mr Gay Pride' award. Louise felt duty-bound to express a desire that her shambolic younger sister make a success of it out west . . . but found she only harboured a desire to anchor Jane with weights in a piranha-packed jacuzzi. Jane, on the other hand, felt sure that if her perfectionist, control-freak older sister ever ended up in a lifeboat, the other passengers would eat her by the end of the first day, even if they had plenty of food and water and land was in sight, just because she was so bloody annoying.

'But where?' Louise stepped gingerly over the dog turds

that polka-dotted the pavement. Insisting on dwelling in this slum area when Jane could have bought a nice house in the inner west for half the price with their parent's inheritance was typical of little sister's perversity. 'Where are you going, if it's not too much to ask?'

'Broken Ridge. Mining town.' Jane leant on the car chassis to catch her breath. Hands on stout, denim-clad hips, she faced her svelte, designer-suited sister. 'I've been on so many blind dates, I should be given a free dog. But all the time, I've been looking in the wrong bloody places.' Her face became vivid with excitement. 'In the outback,' she chirped, 'men outnumber women ten to one.' She retrieved a scrunched-up newspaper article from her jeans pocket.

Louise perched her sunglasses on top of her highlighted blonde bouffant, smoothed out the blurred print with her manicured claws and read aloud.

'A mayor in the outback has called on "beauty-disadvantaged" ladies to move to his town, where a woman shortage means that the men aren't too picky. "Quite often you will see walking down the street a lass who is not so attractive with a wide smile on her face. Maybe a recollection of something previous, or anticipation for the next evening? . . . If you're an ugly duckling, why not move here and evolve into a beautiful swan?"'

Louise glanced at her sister. Jane had hope all over her – she was positively perfumed by it. Louise's face, however, was a knot of opinion. 'It's appalling! To judge women by how they look! What about personality? And IQ? You're so clever and funny, Jane.'

'So bloody what?' Jane replied tightly, her smile evaporating. 'Any bloke who ever liked my sense of humour ended up falling in love with *you*.' She regarded her older sister with slant-eyed hostility.

A passerby would not have picked them as sisters. Whereas Louise glided, Jane loped. While Louise was coltish, with a swimmer's body, the hammocks of flesh under Jane's mottled upper arms wobbled as she gesticulated. While Louise was fine-featured (although Jane secretly thought her older sister's proboscis a little hawk-like, which gave her a predatory air) Jane knew that her own soft knob of a nose was lost on her big-boned face, as though stuck on with Blu-tack.

'Women are as close to being appreciated for our personalities as Garry Glitter is of getting a job in a frigging nursery school,' Jane concluded bitterly.

'But you're very attractive, Jane – in your own way.'

Jane's face flushed elusive expressions before narrowing into a look of contempt. 'Oh puh-lease. Don't treat me like a child. Do you think Mum knew I was going to be plain? She took one look in the crib and thought – plain Jane.'

Uncomfortable with the familiar turn their talk was taking, Louise conversationally tacked. '"Beauty-disadvantaged!" God, that must make the women in the town feel so special.'

Jane shrugged. 'I dunno. I think the mayor is being quite pragmatic.'

'He's facially prejudiced,' Louise crisply enunciated, as if addressing an invisible jury.

Jane's eyes glittered with spite. 'Oh, and you're not? You judge *your* man by *his* looks. You once said to me, "No pecs, no sex". And anyway, Travis, your live-in Ken doll, *he* judges *you*. Do you think he'd be living with you if you looked like *me*?'

Louise took a deep breath and then employed the reasonable tone she used to calm traffic wardens and hostile witnesses. 'I know you've taken against Travis, but you're wrong. He's a—'

'. . . shallow, superficial snob. Along with Vlad the Impaler and Robert Mugabe, Travis would be eliminated early in the heats for Mr Caring and Sharing.'

Louise's anger boiled over like milk. 'That's just not true! You have no idea how much Travis does for human rights!'

'Hey, one appearance at a charity ball for Amnesty does not a human rights lawyer make.'

'You're talking about the man I love!'

'Well, you obviously have so much in common because he's in love with himself, too,' Jane added mulishly.

It was now Louise's turn to look at her little sister with thin-lipped disapproval. 'You're just jealous. Ever since we were teenagers, you've had enough chips on your shoulder to open a casino. Can't you just be happy for me?'

'Gee, I dunno, sis. It's just that seeing two such perfect people united in mutual adoration makes me experience something I've never felt before – nausea to the point of projectile vomiting. Now, if you'll excuse me. I have a husband to hunt.'

Louise placed an urgent, restraining hand on her sister's elbow. 'You can't just up and leave, Jane. What about your students? Your friends? Your job at the con? You always wanted to teach at the conservatorium . . .'

'Yeah . . . My life's so busy, what with the sale at Target and the dishwasher filter needing changing.'

'You can't just hunt down a husband. It's not like shopping for a pair of shoes! Even Cinderella had to wait for the right glass slipper to come along.'

'J'know, taking lessons on love from you is like taking ballroom dancing classes from al-Qaeda. I'm going, and that's all there is to it.'

'No you are *not*!' Louise seized her sister's other arm and held her tight. 'I mean, think it through. The truth about finding a man in the outback is that the odds are good – but the goods are odd.'

'How the fuck would you know? You've never bloody well been out there!' Jane broke free, her face shattering like glass. 'You're just judging the place on appearances, as usual. At least there are blokes out there – and any bloke is better than no bloke. Bloody hell. I've got so many Rampant Rabbit vibrators they need their own warren.'

'Ah . . . I hate to break it to you, but I don't think that's what's meant by the rabbit-proof fence,' Louise punned superciliously.

'It's not funny! I've worn off a fingerprint.' Jane waggled her fingers in her sister's face. 'I could perform the perfect crime, now.'

'Well you'll be in good company. You know what kind of men are in the outback? Felons and misfits, rednecks and renegades.' Louise barred her sister's access to the driver's door with her body. 'Men like Ivan Milat and the monster who killed that poor Falconio boy. In fact, I can't believe that Extreme Sports Enthusiasts haven't taken up husband hunting in the outback as the ultimate risk-taking thrill.'

'You're not listening to me! I'm sick of being marooned by the pretzels at parties, playing Spot the Hetero.' Sadness flowed down Jane's face, from her brow to her mouth. 'My girlfriends and I squabble over any man who still has his own teeth!' Her voice was like a wasp in a jar. 'I've done everything but wear Fosters-flavoured lip gloss. And still nothing!'

'I'm sorry you haven't been lucky in love. But face facts, Jane! Rednecks will shag anything. Including warm pies or tethered, reasonably domesticated livestock.'

'You really do exceed one hundred per cent of the recommended daily allowance of Smug, Louise. Now move!' The sturdily built Jane flicked her delicate sister out of her way as though she were a fly.

Louise's nerves were now shrieking louder than the unoiled hinges of Jane's vintage car door. 'You can't go!' It came out as a barked command. 'Answer this mayor's request and you're admitting you're desperate.' Louise shoved her head through the passenger window. 'Where is your dignity?'

Jane scoffed, her expression vinegary. 'Dignity's a superfluous emotion for plain women. Like hair gel for bald men. Bye.' She gunned the motor. Louise just had time to jump back as the car lurched from the curb.

Though she was fuming, Louise knew it wouldn't last. Just like all Jane's other hair-brained schemes – saving the Tasmanian rainforest, helping the tsunami victims, raising lion cubs in Africa.

On the taxi ride home through the leafy tranquillity of the North Shore, Louise wondered how anyone could contemplate finding a husband in the outback, where the monosyllabic men just whistle or beep as they pass – the sort of communication skills women just adore. When her sister skulked back into town, with her trousseau between her legs, Louise would have to try hard not to have an attack of the 'I told you so's'. Two weeks – that's all she gave it.

• •

When the wedding invitation plopped through the letter-box one month later, Louise flumped back onto the sofa in a fugue of shock, her eyes bare and round as light bulbs. She made a noise like a tyre going flat. Jane? Married! Louise just couldn't believe her sister was going to beat her down the aisle. And with a Neanderthal.

'A redneck brother-in-law. Oh, a dream come true,' Travis droned. 'I didn't think Jane even *liked* the Great Outdoors, with all its multi-footed insects.'

'Ah, but she does like getting bitten all over by eligible men . . . And unfortunately the best place to find eligible men is in the Great Outdoors. It's the snooze alarm. It's gone off on her biological clock.'

'But she's only known the man for a month. Where did she find him? A fiancé-vending machine?' Travis put down his Italian leather briefcase and unknotted his Armani tie. 'He's obviously only after her money. She must have told him about her inheritance.'

'I tell you what, if our parents hadn't died in that dreadful helicopter accident, their daughter marrying a gold-digging low-life would have killed them anyway.' Louise handed him a glass of creamy chardonnay. 'My sister's wedding vows should state: "Do you take this woman to the cleaners, for fifty per cent of her income, from this day forth, for richer and richer? You bloody well bet I do! I now pronounce you Man and Mansion."' Louise's heart gave a wrench of protective love. 'We've got to stop them.'

'The outback?' Travis shuddered. 'Great place to visit – if you're a sheep. Why is it that while beasts of the field, birds, invertebrates even, all pair off happily without the aid of speed dating and internet love sites listing GSOHs, the human species needs inducements from country mayors and the like to mate? We didn't need any help getting together.' He drew her towards him for a soft, lingering kiss.

For Louise and Travis it had been love at first sight. She'd adored him since the day she accidentally ate Exhibit A. She'd been waiting in his chambers to discuss a brief and consumed the evidence – a piece of chocolate. Instead of throwing her off the case, Travis merely commented that any judge would go ahead and hold her in contempt – or just hold her. They slept together that night.

Louise looked up at her fiancé as he swept his hands through a schoolboy head of dark, floppy hair that fell over his forehead in a sweep. His smile was so bright it could act as a beacon for round-the-world yachtsmen adrift in the ocean. He flashed it at her now as he unbuttoned his shirt and flexed his toned muscles – musculature last seen on Michelangelo's *David*. In fact, the man looked positively underdressed without a plinth. He ran his hand up under her skirt while looking into her eyes. Travis's even-featured profile, square jaw and black-rimmed glasses always made her think of Clark Kent, an image emphasised by the fact that he was so earnest, go-getting and immaculately pin-stripe-shirted by day, then wild and Caped-Crusaderish by night. Removing his spectacles was Travis's sign that he was in the mood to go over to the Dark Side ... After one particularly wild ride, they'd nicknamed each other Ophthalmic and Louise.

She watched him place his glasses on the coffee table and, taking her cue, shrugged herself deeper into his arms, inhaling his familiar aroma as he pulled her down onto the shag pile.

Afterwards, they lay entwined on the living-room floor as if their limbs had been deliberately fashioned for an advertisement shoot. The waves of Neutral Bay lapped the rocks below their harbourside apartment – a glass cube suspended over an infinity pool. 'An infinity pool? Oh, where will it all end?' Travis had quipped the day they'd put down the deposit.

'So I'll book flights for Friday then, shall I?' The February sunlight flickered through the potted palm fronds. Despite the serenity, she felt her boyfriend's body stiffen.

'The outback contains large quantities of nature, doesn't it?' he winced. 'If a single, heterosexual man in Sydney really *is* harder to find than Melanie Griffith's birth certificate, then maybe you should just let Jane go.'

'The best thing about having a sister, Travis, is that when you don't know what you're doing, there is always someone who does. In our teens, I stopped Jane from going out with more ineligible blokes than I care to remember!'

'But being single in your thirties probably does recalibrate one's view of eligible, Lou Lou.'

Louise gave her future husband a flat, measuring look. 'So, I take it you're not coming with me?'

'Think about it, babe. If I walk through a bar door in a mining town, I'll accidentally set off the Wanker City Lawyer Detector and get pulverised. Besides, I have so much work to do. I'm sure you'll do what's best for that sad sister of yours.' Travis was shaking his head sympathetically, but from a great distance. He was already thinking about his case. Louise often joked that she suffered from subpoena envy – but found herself momentarily annoyed by his workaholism.

'Besides, you'll be back in a day.' There was a smug note of certainty in his voice. 'Jane's just trying to one-up you. There probably is no . . .' he snatched the invitation up from the floor where Louise had tossed it, 'Bill Jackman.' Travis gave a little hiss of amusement. 'And even with an imaginary friend, one look at your sister naked and it will all be over!'

'Jane's not that bad looking, Travis.'

'I know . . . It's just that she will insist on using her body as a repository for fast food. She should take a heavily pregnant woman with her everywhere she goes to make her look slimmer.' Travis tsk-ed his tongue and sighed, stroking Louise's flank. '*I* won the genetic lottery though, didn't I? Sometimes I just can't believe you're not adopted.'

Louise smiled indulgently at her husband-to-be and nestled securely into the crook of his arm, like a baby.

• •

When Louise first saw the town her sister intended to make her home, it was hate at first sight. It was hard to say what she hated more. Was it the heat? The air was so dry the trees were positively whistling for dogs. The chooks would be laying hard-boiled eggs. Was it the 'super pit', which seemed as vast and deep as the Grand Canyon? Gargantuan trucks, each wheel the size of a seaside bungalow, laboured, ant-like, up and down its raw, red slopes day in, day out. Or was it the Aboriginal settlement, comprising windowless dormitories, situated between two pits – the sewage and the super? No, surely it was the casual racism? 'What did Jesus say to the Abbos when he was up on the cross?' her driver bantered, his buttocks spilling over the bucket seat of his taxi. 'Don't do anything till I get back!' More unnerving, still, was the abundance of bars and brothels, which, her driver bragged, were open 'twenty-four/seven' to accommodate the men on shift work. 'They offer around-the-cock service,' he guffawed, running his bitten nails through a sparse, coppery comb-over. 'Those girls are working away at, well, beaver pitch!'

Louise crossed her legs primly and pursed her mouth into a moue of disgust. What on earth had her irrespon-sible, erratic sister got herself into?

ɪne driver gunned the taxi past what he called the 'starting stalls'. These turned out to be a row of corrugated tin cubicles, in which women sat, semi-clad, in provocative poses awaiting customers. It was like a rustic, rusty, rundown Aussie version of Amsterdam's red light district. Her driver wound down his window and called out to the girls, 'Show us yer pink bits.'

'Gee, I just can't imagine why there's a shortage of women here,' Louise said, churlishly. 'So, what are the criteria you're looking for in a female . . . companion?'

'You just gotta be breathing,' came his romantic reply.

The driver dropped her outside a bar called the Lucky Shag. As Louise fished in her purse, he promised her a T-shirt if she had a drink at all of the town's forty bars. Louise shuddered. There was, no doubt, also a matching underpant for quenching one's erotic thirst at every brothel. He leant out of the taxi window to tuck his card into her bra strap. 'Ring me, sugar tits,' he leered, before revving away.

'And you wonder why you're single?' she seethed in a fug of exhaust fumes.

The relentless blue sky screeched down at her. The whole strident town seemed to bray like a drunken bloke guffawing too loudly at a party. To avoid the broiling heat she retreated, as instructed by Jane, into a hostelry called Skimpy's. It was the kind of bar where even the water is watered down.

The cacophony of male voices that greeted her sounded like a hippo giving birth. Wishing she'd mastered the art of levitation, Louise balanced on the edge of a stool and jiggled her foot with irritation. As her eyes adjusted to the gloom, she understood the pub's name, as the barmaids were wearing the skimpiest underwear imaginable. They were the opposite of icebergs – ninety per cent of them was visible. The customer on her right flipped a two-dollar coin and called 'heads'. Having won the toss, the bored barmaid lifted her top and nonchalantly flashed her bare breasts. The man on Louise's left, who was wearing a shirt that read 'I got crabs at Big Dick's', lost the toss and the barmaid got to keep his coin. Louise's spirits fell even further. It was clear that the only support a woman got in this town was from her wonder bra.

What on earth was her sister doing here? ... The answer to that question arrived on cue. Dear God, don't let that be him, Louise thought, as he gangled in the door, all legs and elbows. She turned back to the bar but soon felt the man's gaze like a breath on the nape of her neck. Boots rang out on the naked wooden floorboards as he strode towards her.

In wide, skidding, languorous vowels the object of her sister's affections said, 'You must be Lou.'

'...*ease*...' She squeezed as much hauteur into her voice as humanly possible. ' Lou*ise*.'

He took off his Akubra to reveal a spriggy black cowlick. 'I'm Jacko.'

Narrowing her eyes with keen interest, Louise surveyed her potential brother-in-law. Bill Jackman was the opposite of what was usually required for the role of romantic hero. In weathered riding boots and regulation moleskins, he was too tall, at about six four. His shirt stuck like a khaki skin, revealing a powerfully built body, but the muscular, mahogany flesh (milk white from the biceps up and neck down) was matted with hair. Tufts sprouted from the open V of his shirt. His face seemed to have been carved by a trainee sculptor. Individually the features were attractive but together they appeared misaligned. Acne scars corrugated his cheeks. Stubble worked through the cratered surface around his broken nose.

'Apparently you've decided to *marry*', she imbued the word with utter contempt, 'my sister after only knowing her for four weeks. You can understand that this makes me decidedly uneasy, as we know nothing about you.' Louise selected 'patronising' from her Roladex of facial expressions. 'Do you have any convictions?'

Jacko gave a playful smirk. 'Nope . . . but you obviously do. That all men are bastards.'

'No,' she bridled. ' I mean *prior* convictions.'

'Yeah, that all the blokes you met *prior* to your fiancé are bastards too. He's a lawyer, right?' Jacko picked up her suitcase. 'Must be fun teasing him about his tiny gavel. Comes in bloody handy as a meat tenderiser, too, I imagine. Or a murder weapon when the uppity bastard gets too pompous,' he winked.

Louise looked at her future brother-in-law with the kind of expression you'd give an incontinent nudist who'd just relieved himself on your bridal gown. She flounced outside, only to be stopped short by the utility truck before her. Actually, Louise wasn't sure if it was a truck or the Starship Enterprise, as it sported enough antennae to get to Mars and back. 'Mr Jackson, you can understand my reticence. And why I need to pry. I hope you don't mind me asking,' she eyed his vehicle with undisguised antipathy, 'but what exactly are your prospects?'

Jacko let out a chuff of laughter. 'I'm a miner, love. I have prospects all over the bloody place!' He swung her small leopard-skin suitcase into the back of the utility truck, where it sat incongruously alongside tools, tarpaulins and a tethered motorbike. 'But I do an honest day's work. Not like those metrosexual knobs and total tossbags in town.'

Louise's eyebrows shot up onto her forehead with finicky disdain. Ignoring his helpful hand, she hauled herself into the passenger seat and orchestrated her linen dress around her knees. Jacko vaulted into the driver's seat and speared the key into the ignition.

'Its only natural that I feel protective towards my little sister,' Louise explained, her expression pinched. 'She is extremely impulsive . . .'

'Don't you ever act on impulse, Lou-*ease*?' Jacko gave a mutinous laugh, lacing his fingers behind his neck and flexing his massive arm muscles in a nonchalant stretch before pulling away from the curb. 'Thinking's overrated, if yer ask me.'

'Human beings are not just a mass of impulses, Mr Jackson. So, what exactly are your intentions?' The word 'intentions' held all the fastidious displeasure of a Victorian aunt.

'I intend to make your sister very, very happy.' He gave her another impertinent wink and drove at a leisurely pace down the wide red road, waving to passersby and hooting his horn in greeting occasionally.

'Oh yes? And exactly how do you plan to do that?' Louise's voice was clipped and precise. 'You're taking her away from her friends, her life, her job. And for what?' There was a crisp reprimand in her voice that forbade contradiction. 'To make her live *here*?' She gestured at the ramshackle town scribbled around the gaping mine. 'In this racist, sexist hellhole?'

Jacko cast an amused eye over Louise and then, to her surprise, laughed right out loud. 'Sure, the blokes around here are rough, but at least what you see is what you get. Those city blokes only call themselves "male feminists" in the hope of getting a more intelligent root.'

They were churning out of town now, through scorched countryside. A recent bushfire had left a black calligraphy of trees scratched into the landscape. The utility truck lurched into gravelled depressions, the wheels noisily throwing up dirt.

'What else can I make of a town that calls the seam of gold you mine "The Body"? What kind of image does that conjure? A geological Elle Macpherson, crawling with men,' Louise cringed.

Jacko gave a rich chuckle. 'But in a town with one female to every ten blokes, it's surely the women who are "sitting on a goldmine".'

Louise gave him a narrow look of contempt. 'Yes, your mayor has made that perfectly clear,' she said with exaggerated archness. 'It's obscene – luring plain, vulnerable women out here on the pretext of love, when in reality you just can't be bothered to pay for a prostitute.'

Jacko gave her a polite but sullen look. 'Steady on. We're not that bad. Contrary to the stereotype, we country blokes don't have sex with anything with a hole and a heartbeat. Company. That's what we crave. Naw, it's the city fellas you gotta worry about. They've got youse women starving yourselves and cutting your faces to stay young and beautiful . . . Jane reckons if your boyfriend told you to only eat pedicure shavings for a more invigorated complexion, you'd damn well do it. Skin has only one function, yer know, Louise. To stop your insides from slopping out all over the place . . . But it'll no doubt take you two thousand diets and twenty-eight surgical procedures to realise that you'd be much more beautiful if you read a book now and then. Jane . . . now, *there's* a reader,' he concluded fondly.

This unexpected diatribe left Louise shaking all over, like a dog taunted by bees. Okay, the man had more communication skills than she'd anticipated, but how dare he talk to her that way! She forced a smile, but it was sharp as a razor. 'The truth is, Mr Jackson, I don't need to be informed of my sister's many and wonderful qualities. It's just totally beyond me what *she* sees in *you*. Jane is an artist. She plays the cello beautifully. But with you, all I hear is the sound of barrels being scraped.'

'Is that right?' Jacko dodged a lump of fetid road kill. 'The way I look at it is, I'm a human being first and a Love God second . . . But really? Am I that unattractive? At the mine, my shower window looks into the window of the women's changing rooms. I've been meaning to get a blind but, hey, why spoil their view?'

Louise refused to be amused and bestowed on him the kind of superior look that could have got her the part of an extra in a Dracula movie.

'Anyway, j'know why it's better to go out with an ugly bloke? We're so damn grateful, which makes us less demanding . . . I suppose your legal eagle fella can only enjoy sex if he pretends it's a conjugal visit.' He laughed as the ute moaned its way up an incline.

As they crested the hill, the barrage of barbed retorts on the tip of Louise's tongue was silenced by the sight of a huge male kangaroo bounding right into their path. Louise spasmed with fear, a scream in her blood. Jacko spun the wheel; the car lurched sideways, hit something solid and rolled. The windscreen winced at the impact then shattered. Terror exploded onto the screen of Louise's eyelids. There was a smell of burning rubber followed by the full-throated roar of a car crumpling like a cigarette packet. The earth and sky blurred, and then the world imploded. Louise was aware of smashing glass tinkling like waves on shingle. And then the world went black.

• •

Louise felt herself clawing back into consciousness. Fibres of light crawled into her cranium. She opened her eyes to find she was lying flat on a blanket under a shrub flannelled in dust. The sting of blood was in her sinuses. Each ragged breath felt like inhaling fire but the elation of being alive engulfed her.

A belch of petrol breath alerted her to the demolished ute, up-ended. The aftershock reverberated through her body and a bubble of hysteria rose in her chest.

Jacko, on the other hand, had erupted into a great nonchalance. 'Bloody hell, eh?' was all he said. He was sponging dirt off her skin and checking for wounds. 'You've been out for the count for yonks. I've called for help. Jane's on her way. Are you okay?' Louise now noted that, despite Jacko's surface calm, his skin had gone the colour of a cold Sunday roast. When she nodded, Jacko's smile broke on her like a wave on a beach. 'Here, take this for the pain.'

Cupping her head, he helped her gulp down some pills. As the drugs kicked in, a spreading, pleasurable sensation flowed over her like melting butter. Surprised into acquiescence, she became as docile as a child, allowing the miner to pull open her clothes. The sun and shade made a mosaic of light and shadow on his face.

Jacko had fashioned a makeshift shelter from a tent pole and a tarpaulin. She found herself intrigued by this durable man, with his first-aid kit and Harley Davidson – Travis would need trainer wheels on such a powerful motorbike. It crossed her mind that she'd only once asked Travis to perform some DIY and he'd reacted as though she'd asked him to fuel a nuclear reactor. Jacko, on the other hand, was the type of bloke who could take a cold capsule and still operate heavy machinery. Senses enhanced, she inhaled his warm spicy scent – a musky tang of petrol, sweat and cigarettes. Looking at him, through the prism of painkillers, it suddenly didn't seem so strange to find him loveable. The nose she'd found coarse now appeared Romanesque. The broad features, chiselled. He wasn't gym-toned, like Travis, but corded by the kind of bulging muscles and sinews that only came from hard physical labour. And yet the strength of his body was so at odds with his velvety fingertips.

'Your hands are so soft,' she marvelled.

'Shearing. It's the lanolin – in the wool. You're so lucky, Lou. These abrasions are only superficial.'

Bandaging a cut on her upper arm, his hand grazed the pillowy softness of her breast. Oddly enchanted, she was astonished by a fierce rush of tenderness. The stillness of the outback was like an audience hushed in anticipation. But her mind was electric, filled with the present and the hot and resinous perfume of the bush. A languorous sensuality took hold. The air felt solid, the weight of it pressing down on her. She tilted her face up to him, like a sunflower turning towards the heat. As if drawn by the inexorable pull of a thread, she slowly inclined her head upwards, drifting in a trance-like state towards his mouth.

The torniqueted quiet was loud enough to make her open her eyes. The look on Jacko's face registered more surprise than the congregation at Michael Jackson's wedding. He leapt back as though from the strike of a cobra. When he spoke it was from lips no more than a crack between the nose and chin.

'Your sister is a truly beautiful person,' was all he said.

'Yes. She is. Of course,' Louise blurted, snapping out of her reverie, her voice light and falsely cheery. The extent of the man's rejection impacted like a blow to her chest. A kookaburra cackled with derision. At the low-throated rumble of an approaching car, Louise felt a knot of remorse in her stomach. She wanted to remind Jacko that he'd said thinking was overrated and to go with her impulses, but his eyes were unreadable beneath the brim of his hat, his body language tense, his fury monumental.

Jane leapt from the Mustang with the wheels still spinning. Once she realised Louise was okay, she laughed with giddy abandon, her arms warm around her sister's neck.

'I'm fine. Really. Fine.' Louise's voice was all staccato stoicism.

The face Jane turned to Jacko was naked in its love.

• •

On the drive to the hospital, Louise could hear her sister babbling happily, a brook of words, her laughter vibrant with affection and relief. Louise forced a smile – a smile as sharp and sweet as icing and as lacquered as the nails she was digging into her palm. Why had she tried to kiss him? She was engaged to the most perfect man on the planet. Louise, normally so clear-sighted, found that everything had blurred slightly. It was the shock of the crash, obviously. But that didn't stop her feeling that Jane had become the swan and she the ugly duckling. And as soon as Jacko told Jane, things would get very ugly indeed.

After the all-clear from the hospital and still unable to reach Travis on his mobile, Louise collapsed into an old wrought-iron bed on Jacko's sheep station. His quaint wooden farmhouse was slightly tilted, as though tipsy, and the corrugated iron of the roof creaked companionably in the wind. Full of books and paintings and sculptures, a Boccherini quintet playing softly, it was not what Louise had expected at all. She woke in the morning to the sound of her sister laughing, and looked into the courtyard below to see Jane making extravagant gestures to accentuate her animated anecdotes, at which Jacko laughed delightedly. Louise joined them with trepidation.

Over brunch, Jacko's luminous eyes fleetingly held Louise's – a look of polite contempt. But Jane's eyes stayed summery with laughter, meaning he hadn't told her of his close encounter of the Lady Chatterley kind. The light around Jane seemed warmer somehow. Alluring. Strolling by the creek, Louise and Jane smiled at each other in a tentative way. No longer adversaries, they were unsure how to speak to each other.

'I really must write to Shirley MacLaine,' Louise joshed. 'You are the first woman in the world who has been reincarnated *while still alive*.'

On Sunday Jacko met up with his mates, some of whom were Aboriginal, to take part in what they called the Undie 500. The miners she'd dismissed as selfish, racist yobs had dyed their hair red, blue, green and yellow to raise money for a children's cancer charity and had been sponsored to drive around all day in just their undies. Louise laughed, finally starting to appreciate the local humour, which was drier, she now realised, than the encroaching desert.

Driving to the airport later on, the town itself didn't look as bad as it had at first sight. The pub verandahs were delicately fringed with iron lace. The streets, built wide and expansive to accommodate a full bullock dray as it turned, were Russell Drysdale without the angst. The red earth and blue sky gave the place a surreal quality. Louise found herself glancing around the landscape expecting to see a Daliesque dripping clock or a melting face on stilts.

At the check-in desk, Jane embraced Louise then thumped Jacko in the arm. 'He's an ugly bugger but, hey, you can't always judge by appearances.' At which Jacko barked an irreverent laugh.

'At least you can no longer say that all the men who ever liked your sense of humour ended up fancying me,' Louise said, glancing tentatively at Jacko.

'And anyways,' Jacko philosophised good-naturedly, staring right back at Louise, 'ugliness is in the eye of the beholder. Get it out with Visine.'

Rough diamonds were all very well, Louise thought to herself as she settled into her airline seat, but she liked hers with a little polish. After her outback misadventure, she couldn't wait to get back to her beloved.

• •

In her absence Sydney seemed to have metamorphosed from sparkling gem to zircon. The city, smeared in car fumes, lay in an indolent light beneath burnished tower blocks. Pedestrians hurried by like caged mice.

'Darling!' Travis looked up from his spotless plexiglas study desk, which looked, now Louise thought about it, like a glass case in a museum.

She was about to recount the details of her accident when Travis interrupted. 'Notice anything?' He leant back in his ergonomically correct chair. 'No glasses!' he said, before she could answer. 'I had my eyes lasered. It's almost Biblical . . . I can see! I can see!'

'But I liked your glasses,' Louise said, baffled. 'Ophthalmic and Louise, remember? Why didn't you ask me?'

'I wanted it to be a little surprise.'

'But you said you were working! Is that why you didn't come with me to find Jane?'

'Well, yes, actually . . . What do you think?'

What Louise thought was that their neo-modern, earth-toned apartment lacked character. It was seared by light yet freezing cold, the thermostat set to Polar Expedition. She missed the soporific heat and outback air thick with the abundant birds and insects.

'And to tell the truth, I wasn't entirely convinced about your mission, Lou Lou. The man may be a redneck, but to be frank, with Jane's looks, I thought all she'd ever have between her legs is a cello.'

'Jane is a highly intelligent, artistic woman. Are looks all that count to you men? When they say beauty comes from within, Travis, they do not mean from within a jar marked "Estee Lauder".'

'Okay, okay. I take it back,' Travis said blithely. 'I think you're just a little tired after your trip out to that hellhole.' He massaged her shoulders. 'How hellish was it?'

'Actually, it has its own beauty – the bush.'

Travis slid her dress off her shoulders and nibbled her neck. 'Not as beautiful as you. Let's make love, right here, looking out over the harbour.' He knelt to peel down her panties but his head jerked back like a snake surprised by a mirror. 'Is that . . . is that . . . cellulite? Good God, I never noticed that before.' Louise's fiancé began to examine her thighs with such intensity she felt like a new strain of bacteria beneath a microscope. 'How long have you had cellulite . . . ?' he asked playfully, but his gaze was reproachful. 'Come to think of it, I've never really seen you naked. My eyesight was so bad. And I always took my glasses off when we made love. Well, well, well. Who's been letting herself go?' He addressed her as though she were a stray cat that had wandered into the garden.

Louise felt a shift in her feelings for her fiancé. It was as though she'd woken up to find that all the furniture in her flat had been rearranged. Before she had time to reorientate, Travis pulled her down onto the carpet by his study mirror. 'My word, Lou Lou, what were they feeding you out there?' He gave her three pats on her rump, like you would give an old dog. 'Somebody needs to tone up! Now that I've had laser surgery, there's no pulling the wool over my eyes any more, eh?'

The man she thought she adored began to go a little blurry, like a smudged watercolour, or a photo slightly out of focus. Travis made love to her with his usual athleticism, but the liaison took on the weighty, soft-boned weariness of anaesthetic.

Afterwards, when she glanced across at him to gauge his reaction to the slight bruises and scratches on her upper arms, Travis was looking at her as though she were a carb-laden, full-fat burger his doctor had told him to avoid, instead of the organic beet salad he'd actually ordered. 'Perhaps you need a better jogging bra, babe. Haven't you noticed those stretch marks on your breasts? I've never noticed them before.' His tone was one of baffled disappointment.

Thoughts crowded her mind like traffic. 'One day I will have nipples on my knees, you know. What will you think then?'

'There's always cosmetic surgery. Beauty is, after all, one of the most natural and lovely things money can buy,' he joshed, but there was no warmth in his voice.

'I see. So, are our wedding vows going to say "For better or for worse – but not if your secretary is prettier and predatory?"'

'Of course not, darling,' he said, but his smile did not quite reach his eyes. He pulled her to him again and plant-ed some conciliatory kisses on her nipples.

She attempted a caress in return, but her lover seemed to be disappearing before her eyes, melting slowly, like a snowman, until all that was left of him was a pool of ice. As he entered her from behind, she glanced up over her shoulder and caught Travis looking appreciatively into the mirror – at himself. It was then that her mild anxiety morphed into revulsion. She couldn't suppress a swift shudder of disgust. Epiphany was the word she would use later to friends. Her fiancé obviously kept fit by doing step aerobics off his own ego. Her sister was right. The man had love bites on his mirror. Travis may have had the eye surgery, but it was Louise's vision that was suddenly, miraculously clear. They'd been so keen to get an apartment that overlooked the harbour, yet they had overlooked each other. In the evening sun, the harbour became a shining mirror – and she didn't like what she saw – namely, that her abrasions were not the only superficial thing about her. She'd been emotionally myopic – psychologically shortsighted. Blind. *She* was the one in need of glasses. The waves became hard, reprimanding smacks against the shore.

Travis stopped stroking her thigh and flicked at a patch of dry skin. 'Maybe you need a body scrub, babe? Or a day at the spa or something?'

Her angry expression evaporated into a look of distant, almost sweet, abstraction. 'Really? My clever sister has found the perfect cure for that. Lanolin.' She slapped away his hand and sashayed across the room to snap off the aircon and throw open the window. 'Oh, and a little hint to help you find your next girlfriend, Travis. Ugliness is in the eye of the beholder . . . Get it out with Visine.'

3

Life in a Hotel Room

William McInnes

The movie star and her movie star husband smiled their movie star smiles as they held each other. Her lips were the size of life rafts and his were no better. The accountant was surprised he could see the dentist's work and that their teeth were so white. They were on a red carpet in a city at the other end of the world.

It was the launch of the movie star's new fragrance, Africa. She'd dedicated this fragrance to the continent she loved, a fragrance as raw and vital as the continent itself.

The accountant had no real reason to look at the movie stars, except that he couldn't be bothered looking at four-wheel-drives or holiday destinations or gourmet food tours, or any of the other magazines on the little tables in the medical clinic.

It felt more like a bus terminal than a clinic. People sat staring ahead, occasionally coughing or giving the odd sniff and groan or reading the magazines. They were surrounded by bags: shopping bags, travelling bags and work cases.

He wondered whether anybody here would splash a little bit of Africa on themselves.

He didn't think so. He looked at the movie stars again and suddenly remembered that they were no longer together. The male movie star had run off with the couple's nanny. He knew that because the last holiday he took, he saw a magazine cover in a beachside shop that had the news blazing across the cover.

He looked at the date of the magazine. It was over a year old. Recycled waiting-room reading matter. No mind, it was just pictures, anyway.

A lot can change in a year. The accountant knew that. Fear and panic. The Great Recession. The movie stars hadn't even heard of the Great Recession or the Global Financial Crisis. Maybe they hadn't even hired that nanny yet.

Well, it was all ahead of them, thought the accountant.

'Africa,' he said softly.

The receptionist called his name. 'Doctor will see you in room three.'

He nodded and walked on through to the room. As he did, somebody sneezed again.

• •

It was because he was travelling. That was why he was having trouble. That's what he thought. That's what he told the doctor.

'Do you travel much?' asked the doctor as he took the blood pressure reading.

'Yes, quite a bit for work.'

He had flown into Sydney that morning and had been in meetings all day.

'Have you had the trouble before?'

'No. Not really.'

'Well, perhaps it's not the travel. What is it that you do?'

The question he had been dreading.

'I'm an accountant.'

The doctor looked at him.

'An accountant,' he said again. 'A corporate auditor.'

The doctor looked at him.

'And you've been having trouble for . . . how long?'

'Just the past two or three days, no, a week . . . I've been travelling a lot, more than usual. Work has been busy.'

'More so than usual?' asked the doctor.

He had been busy sitting in offices up and down the eastern coast that all looked the same, felt the same and smelt the same. Sitting there with his laptop and his papers filled with figures and tables and statistics that indicated quick and decisive action needed to be taken.

'The cycle indicates quick and decisive action needs to be taken.' That was what he'd said in the offices up and down the eastern coast. The regional director had patted him gently on the shoulder after the last time he said those words.

'Shit, mate, you really are very good at what you do.' And the accountant had nodded. 'We'll send you something around to the hotel, just to say thanks. And sorry about where you're staying, it's the only half-decent one we could get you in. Mardi Gras weekend – place is booked out. Nasty business. Terrible.'

The accountant looked at the regional director.

'The cycle, the action we need to take. Bloody recession.'

And the regional director had patted him again. And the accountant thought, not for the first time, that he wished he could go to the toilet. Or rather, that when he went something would happen. Or that he could sleep.

The accountant looked at the doctor.

'It's been busier than usual,' he said. The cycle had been working overtime. Not his own but the economic one.

The doctor looked at him and nodded.

'And you've had stomach discomfort and your bowel movements are slightly irregular, and your sleep is disturbed.'

The accountant nodded.

'Your blood pressure is relatively high for your age and you're a little bit overweight . . . And you're forty-five?'

The accountant nodded.

'Diabetes is something that may become an issue for you. It's important to try to look after yourself when you don't keep a regular work routine . . .'

'That's why I came here to see you,' said the accountant.

The doctor smiled slightly. He was English and had suitable grey hair and a pleasant manner.

'Well, a doctor can only do so much. Let's see what that might be . . . you may have a blockage, or something even approaching haemorrhoids.'

The accountant stared at him.

'So, I suppose I should have a look to see what you may have.'

'What does that mean?' asked the accountant.

'It means I will have to have a look at your bottom, to examine your bottom. Not the perfect way to end your day, I dare say, but we're just making sure there's nothing amiss.' The doctor smiled.

What it meant was the accountant on the medical table with his arse in the air and there was some snapping of gloves and waiting.

The accountant couldn't escape what he was and where he was.

There comes a time in our travels through life when fingers belonging to a suitably qualified professional may be inserted for the most medical of reasons into the orifice the accountant was now pointing toward the heavens. But the accountant could have handled it better.

Yes, he could have handled it better.

It was because there was no conversation in the room, that's where it began. Just the sounds of the doctor readying himself with the slap of gloves and the slurp of lubricants.

The accountant's voice sounded like somebody else's. 'What are you doing?'

'Just preparing,' said the gloved doctor cheerfully enough.

He had the sort of accent that doctors on British detective television shows have. Those shows the accountant and his family would sit and watch with takeaway food on a Friday night. The accountant knew that those Friday nights in front of the television would never be quite the same again.

The shows where Inspector Midsomer or Miss Marple, or whoever the ex-Shakespearean great is who is performing the TV detective, unmasks the nice, solicitous doctor as the villain of the piece.

They would puff on their pipe. The accountant didn't know if Miss Marple had a pipe but she could always try – maybe Inspector Midsomer could wear a twin set. And nod sagely as the doctor was dragged away.

'And I'd do it all again,' the pleasant doctor would say as he was dragged away and gloves and lubricant were collected by constables.

The TV detective's dim offsider would then say, 'Who would have thought it was the doctor, sir? And that his only weapon was his index finger?'

'Hmmm,' sighs Inspector Hercules-Marple-Midsomer, 'A nasty business.'

They always say, 'A nasty business.' The accountant suddenly remembered that the regional director had used those very words when talking about the GFC.

Index fingers.

'Now I'm just going to carry out the examination,' said the murderous doctor.

From the accountant's childhood came a memory of one of the most gothic and gruesome index fingers.

As a child he had been taken to celebrate Queensland's colonial past at Newstead House, the former residence of imperial governors. The house sat on the banks of the Brisbane River and had been turned into a type of museum. He had wandered through the rooms that were dressed up in the style of the colonial past. There were no people there, just the furniture, and clothes lay on the beds. It was like walking through a ghost house, no life, just the remnants and the reminders of it.

The accountant had been told off by his teacher when the bloody nose he had complained about had been discovered to be the result of the accountant picking at it. A girl in pigtails and braces had told on him. 'I'm going to dob on you!' she had said.

And she did. She dobbed on him for picking his nose and making it bleed. He had skulked up to the front of the line with the teacher's hanky clamped over his nose.

Then came the big talking point of the display. Something that didn't need any dressing up. It was purported to be a convict's finger in formaldehyde in a Masterfoods cayenne pepper bottle.

'Maybe they cut it off because he picked his nose!' boomed the teacher and the girl in pigtails giggled.

'Would you like that finger up your nose?' carried on the teacher.

The accountant thought he didn't want the finger up his nose or up anything. He could still hear that girl with the pigtails laughing.

Then another thought struck him. It was bad enough to be haunted by the visions of some Edgar Allan Poe convict finger about to carry out an examination, but that it was covered in cayenne pepper was too much.

He could have handled it better. It was, as they say, 'A nasty business.'

There in that suite of a twenty-four-hour medical clinic on Broadway he lay and grunted a bit. As soon as he grunted a bit he became embarrassed. The digit stopped.

The good doctor asked, 'Is that causing you discomfort?'

'No. Not at all.'

The doctor coughed softly.

A thought flashed through the accountant's brain. 'Does he think I like it?'

Pitiful really. But as the doctor went about his business the accountant was gripped by the need to make some sort of conversation. At his most vulnerable he grasped at the only branch he could find.

'Debt leverage is what I've been dealing with. Debt and

dealing with the decreasing credit market. It's all relative, all relative to the amount of credit available. As access to credit decreases, the debt increases . . . I . . .'

The finger stopped and then went about its task.

'Then the base, the capital, your actual liquid assets, the cash if you like, shrinks. That's when you've got to downsize the debt. The cycle indicates that decisive action needs to be taken and that means minimising the target. Minimising costs . . . Rationalising your outgoings . . . It's all relative.

'Right, there's nothing really there I can, uh, see,' said the doctor.

The finger withdrew. The accountant couldn't stop. 'The problem, the crisis, if you like, is that people have been finding new ways to tier credit, to make different levels of credit to sell and layer their profits.'

'You can sit up now,' said the doctor.

'They've been selling something that doesn't exist,' said the accountant and he heard his voice echo in the suite. He pulled up his trousers and buckled his belt.

'Well, it's a nasty business you're involved in, all right,' said the doctor.

The accountant stopped and looked at the doctor. He had never thought of himself as being a part of what his laptop and statistics and figures described.

'Everything is all relative really, I suppose,' said the doctor as he dropped the gloves into a bin. 'I take your blood pressure, your weight, I warn you of the risks of developing diabetes if you don't look after yourself. I even look at your bottom to see if there's anything causing you discomfort. You're forty-five. I tell you to watch your life routine. A life routine. You know the life expectancy in the country I was born in? Zimbabwe?'

The accountant looked at the doctor.

'Thirty-seven years for men and thirty-four years for women. They've been living a crisis for years. Can you imagine that? You'd be an old man now . . .'

The accountant said nothing and the doctor wrote out a script for something to help his patient sleep and a laxative. He held out the script to the other man.

'I thought you were English,' said the accountant.

'Trained there,' said the doctor. 'But I grew up in Zim. I used to think we had so much when I was a boy. But you know, maybe we did and maybe we didn't. It seems so long ago now, the change is so great and I certainly can't trust my memory. I suppose it just goes to show you that things aren't always what they seem.'

The accountant smiled, nodded his head and walked through the waiting room where the movie stars and their life-raft lips were now held in the hands of somebody else.

He stood for a moment on the footpath and watched the cars move slowly along the wide street. A couple of shop entrances down from him slept a person with a collection of coats and some plastic bags.

He hailed a few taxis that ignored him the way taxis do after a long day. One eventually stopped. And he eased himself into the car.

The streets were full of people, some perhaps still here from the Mardi Gras. He had been in Sydney at the same time of the year during previous visits and always thought the streets had a feeling of a pleasant hangover.

He sat and thought briefly of how many 45-year-olds there were in Zimbabwe. And then he considered how the homeless always seemed to look so homeless.

• •

The taxi driver was eating something in a foil wrapper. It looked like a cucumber. It was a cucumber.

'What are you eating?' the accountant asked anyway, for he didn't like the silence.

'A cucumber . . . from my back garden.' The taxi driver was Greek, thought the accountant.

'Nice and tasty.'

'Oh, yes.'

The taxi driver took another bite and spoke as he chewed. 'Good for diabetes.'

'Cucumbers?'

'Oh, yes.'

The accountant thought for a moment. 'Did a doctor tell you that?'

'Oh no . . . Somebody with diabetes – my wife's cousin.' A seed fell onto the taxi driver's shirt and he picked at it. 'He tells me he has diabetes so he eats my cucumbers – English not Lebanese. Thick, not the thin ones.'

The taxi driver changed lanes.

'I eat them and I measure my glucose. It goes down.'

'It went down?' asked the accountant.

'It went down,' confirmed the taxi driver, and he beeped his horn for no particular reason. 'It went down.'

The accountant was silent. A nasty business I'm involved in. He had never thought that he was a part of it. Not really. The taxi stopped at an intersection and the accountant saw they were next to a multi-storey building that seemed to be made entirely of glass. A billboard promising an exciting new concept in retail and residential development stood boldly over the top of the empty first floor. 'Opening November 2008.' The building was almost entirely empty.

That was a long time ago, 2008, thought the accountant. The cycle was at work. The silence, he thought, had lasted too long.

'What else do you grow?'

The taxi driver paused for a minute and kissed the air with his lips. 'I like snake beans. Very much.'

'It's good to grow things,' said the accountant.

They waited for the lights to change. Another smaller billboard stood outside a closed newsagent. It was for a lottery. A chance to win a prize of ten million dollars.

'You have your Powerball in?' asked the taxi driver.

'No.'

'I bet once a month for forty years and never win a bloody cent,' said the taxi driver.

'Right.'

The taxi driver nodded and then sniffed. 'My friend. He was a painter. He buys the Opera House lottery ticket every week then one day he is painting and tells his boss that today is the day he is going to win and . . .' The taxi driver beeped his horn at the lights.

'And?'

'And he wins one hundred thousand pounds . . . one hundred thousand.'

'That was a lot of money back then.'

'Lot of money. But he is stupid, he wastes it, in seven years it is all gone. I tell him he's a fool.'

The lights changed and the taxi eased ahead.

'He laughs and keeps on buying the tickets. He thinks he will win again but he never does. But he was a good friend. He signed my papers for me to come here, and I stayed with him. He was a good friend.'

'Is he still buying the lotto tickets?' asked the accountant.

The taxi driver didn't answer for a moment and then sighed. 'He passed away many years ago . . . Twelve, fourteen years ago.'

'I'm sorry.'

The taxi driver shrugged. 'We all die some time. I told him once he has used his luck up.' The driver looked at the accountant. 'And he just laughed. In hospital I went to see him. I bought him a lottery ticket and gave it to him.'

'And?' said the accountant.

'And he didn't win . . . he just laughed . . . all his family just laughed. He used his luck up and he laughs. He was a good friend. A fool, but a happy man.'

The taxi pulled into a driveway of a hotel near Central Station.

The accountant took out a Cabcharge from his wallet. He offered it to the man behind the wheel, but the taxi driver stared ahead.

'When he died he left me an envelope . . . I opened it and inside was a lottery ticket. A gift for me.' He reached into his own wallet and rummaged in a flap of an old piece of leather. He held up an old lottery ticket. 'I never even see if I won, but I keep him close to me. He was a good friend.'

He returned the ticket to his wallet and processed the Cabcharge.

The accountant signed and as he left the taxi the driver stopped him.

'Remember . . . remember . . . the thick cucumbers.'

The accountant just stared. It had been a long week.

• •

He walked through into the lobby and stood at the reception desk with his little black travelling suitcase trailing behind him like a child's trolley. A clerk with an ill-fitting uniform and moustache to match stood poking at a computer.

The accountant waited.

The clerk had eyes only for the terminal in front of his face.

'Be with you in a moment, sir. The system is terribly slow,' said the clerk.

The accountant assumed that the clerk was talking to him. He nodded.

The clerk continued to prod at his computer terminal, so the accountant turned away and looked around the foyer. It was empty except for a lone figure sitting in a square nest of couches a couple of metres away. The accountant looked again. A young man sat in a purple T-shirt with the word *Eternity* written across the chest. His hair was dyed a platinum blond. When the accountant looked a little more closely he saw that the man seemed to be crying.

If he wasn't crying he seemed to be upset.

The accountant looked to the clerk, but the clerk continued to stare at the computer screen and slowly reached out a dubious finger and poked the keyboard as if he were touching a dead body for signs of life.

'Apologies, sir . . . The system.'

The accountant turned back to the foyer and hadn't meant to look at the young man with the platinum hair and purple Eternity T-shirt again, but there was nothing else to look at. He tried to turn away but the young man met his eye.

'I'm sorry,' the young man said. He was Philippino, thought the accountant. 'I'm sorry, but I have to go home. I have to go . . . and I have had the most beautiful weekend.' His voice caught slightly.

The accountant smiled slightly.

'Everybody has been so friendly and kind, everybody. It was the most beautiful weekend.'

From behind the desk came a tapping noise. The accountant turned to see the clerk tapping the computer with a ruler.

'We are nearly there, sir,' said the clerk, as if he were trying to land a spacecraft on Mars.

'I'm leaving my hair like this. I don't care,' said the young man. 'I have to fly home, but I don't care, it was the most beautiful weekend.'

The accountant looked down at the bag of the young man with the platinum hair. It was a striped plastic bag the colours of the rainbow.

'Where's home?' asked the accountant.

The young man looked up at him and half-smiled.

'Manila, my home is in Manila. I am flying out tonight. I just want to sit and remember my weekend.'

The accountant saw the young man's clothes were tailored in the manner of a more expensive brand than they actually were. He knew this because one of the first steps his company had taken to meet the cycle's demand for quick and decisive action was to close down the offshore factories that produced clothes that looked like more expensive brands. Those off-shore factories were in places like Manila.

'I am so sorry, sir. Would you like to check in?' said the clerk from behind the desk.

The accountant turned and nodded. He handed over his credit card and saw it was the colour of the young man's hair.

'You have a parcel here for you, sir,' said the clerk. His moustache seemed to want to belong to another lip.

'Thank you,' said the accountant. They were just saying thanks for what he had done.

He took the large box and placed it on top of his travelling case and wheeled it over to the lifts. As the doors closed on him he saw the young man with the platinum hair in his nest of couches. The young man held his hand in the air and gently waved. Like the Queen almost, thought the accountant. Or as if he were on a float.

The lift hissed and the accountant closed his eyes. He opened them only when the soft bell told him he had reached his floor. His floor. He had been in so many places with so many His floors and His rooms.

He walked into his room and sat on the bed.

It wasn't the worst of rooms and it wasn't the best.

The accountant sat for a moment longer and then reached for the remote control for the television. He didn't like the silence.

The TV hummed then clicked, and music that sounded like the mood music from his nanna's record collection tinkled away and a message appeared on the screen. The television welcomed him. His name was there on the screen. He sat and looked at the screen and his name. In his room.

He wondered what mood he was supposed to feel.

There was a time when he had thought that a hotel room, with a mini bar and a television, was heaven on a stick.

He remembered that was what his nanna would always say on Boxing Day. When he was a boy his family would spend Boxing Day at his nanna's and she would put her mood music on and bring out a plate of pickled onions and cheese and offer them to her grandchildren with glasses of lime cordial.

'Pickled onions and cheese,' she would croon. 'Heaven on a stick.'

He got off the bed and walked to his mini bar. He opened it. There were no pickled onions and cheese, nothing even remotely like heaven on a stick in there, in that little fridge.

It was true. Mini bars can excite you only for so long. He had reached the point a long time ago when he looked upon the mini bar not so much as a treat and novelty but just as a little fridge with little bottles and long-life milk that tasted like homemade glue.

He looked around his room.

Everything that a person needed. Tiny bottles that cost a bomb and a multi-channelled television with porn movies.

Just why pornographic movies should be a necessary part of a business person's day was never really that clear to him, but the fact you could be assured that the title of the movie would not appear on your bill was in some way seedier than actually watching one.

Watch people having sex and never ever have to admit to it. I'm a business person. I am working.

Except when you have watched one and you settle your bill the next morning and the clerk goes through the bill.

They ask if you have used anything from the mini bar.

They ask if you have watched a movie. Then they see the price. Pornographic movies always cost more so the clerk knows what you watched.

Then the clerk assures the business person, 'The title won't appear on your bill.'

The porn movies, thought the accountant, were never tailored for anyone except men. Straight men. The life of a hotel room has, he thought, too many double standards.

He switched the television to a news channel and watched a breathless American presenter in a carefully concreted hairstyle and clay-pot makeup manicly talk about impending economic doom. The woman didn't even look real. She looked as if she was animated, or rather like a coked-up version of a Thunderbird, from the puppet show from the 1960s.

He was watching a show called *Recession Round-up*.

'Right around the globe we cover the Great Recession,' said the concrete-haired woman.

The accountant switched channels and got an English equivalent Thunderbird talking about the meltdown of the Ukrainian economy.

He tired of the pompous English head and went back to the prattling Yank.

He sat down on his bed and watched the screen. He watched for a time and suddenly realised it wasn't a news network. He had switched to another channel on the television. It was some sort of shopping channel.

The presenters were even more fervent than the news channel Thunderbirds. That made sense to the account-ant. These people were selling things, and what things they were.

The Great Recession may be rolling around the world but nobody would know it, according to these desperate, smiling, eye-popping spruikers. One man was dropping a bowling ball on a pillow with a glass underneath and howling with white-capped delight as the glass was protected by the unique scientific chamber design of the super pillow.

Another man swore that even though he had broken his leg three times playing proball he had never walked straighter, saftier; was that a word, wondered the accountant? It must be, because this grinning cadaver on the television just said it. Had never walked straighter, saftier and with more comfort, thanks to this amazing scientific inner-sole breakthrough.

On and on it went and on and on the accountant watched.

It was only when the testimonials of some happy customers of a revolutionary breakthrough home fitness system began that the accountant turned away.

Would anybody in Zimbabwe be ringing and ordering this?

He took the box that was his present and opened it.

'Jesus Christ,' was all he could manage.

What had his life come to?

He had travelled up and down the east coast of Australia, sitting in offices destroying peoples lives, reaping, he supposed, what he had helped sow. He hadn't slept properly for a week, a doctor had shoved a finger up his arse, and he hadn't crapped properly for as long as he could remember. He sat in a hotel cell and watched people in heavy makeup gabbling about the end of the world as he knew it and now some cross-eyed man with a buzz cut and eyes so close together that they merged into one assured him that, 'My butt is as tight and as firm as it has ever been.'

And now this. His thanks for the job he had been doing. He held in his hands the biggest snow dome he had ever seen. It was the size of a pumpkin.

He held it in front of his face. It was a snow dome of Sydney. The Opera House and Centrepoint and Circular Quay and even the Bridge. Across the skyline in copper-plate lettering was the word *Eternity*.

The accountant shook the snow dome and white particles floated about.

'Jesus,' he said again.

'And my abs are ripped!' said another happy customer to the universe.

A phone rang. The accountant placed the snow dome on the bed and looked at it for a moment, breathed and then muted the television.

He picked up the phone and noted that the people on the television seemed even more insane and desperate when they mouthed noiselessly.

'Hello,' said the accountant.

'Hello,' came a soft little voice from the phone. 'Hello, Daddy.'

His daughter.

'Hello,' he said.

'Hello, Daddy,' she repeated. 'When are you coming home?'

'Tomorrow, I'll be home tomorrow.'

'I want you to come home now.'

The accountant thought of the young man with the platinum hair in the foyer. He was heading home, leaving behind a beautiful weekend.

'Well, I'll be home tomorrow. What's news?'

'I got pupil of the week.'

'Did you? Well done! What was it for?'

'Pupil of the week,' said a perplexed voice.

The accountant laughed for the first time that week. 'I know that, but why were you the pupil of the week?'

His daughter giggled. She would be doing that twirling thing with her left wrist she did when she giggled.

The accountant smiled.

'Well,' said his daughter. 'It says for showing that random acts of kindness are not random, but what the world is meant to be.'

'What?'

'That's what it says.'

'What does that mean?'

His daughter turned away from the phone and he could hear her speak to his wife. 'Mummy, Daddy doesn't know what my award means.'

'That'd be right,' he heard his wife say. 'Give me the phone, sweetie.'

'Hi, darling,' his wife said from the phone.

'Hello. What did she get the award for?'

'There was an old lady who had a bit of a turn in the street and your daughter stayed with her until the ambulance came. Held her hand and chatted to her.'

'Did she know her?'

'No, just some old lady from around here.'

'That's fantastic,' said the accountant.

'Well, you should tell her,' said his wife. 'Here, sweetie, Dad wants to talk to you.'

'Hello,' said his daughter.

'That was ... what you did.' The accountant didn't know what to say.

'Daddy.'

'What you did was very fine.'

'Daddy, she was old, she was scared.'

'Was she?'

'I don't want to be scared when I get older. Are you scared?'

The accountant said nothing.

'Daddy?'

'Not when I talk to you, baby girl.'

'I love you.'

'Not as much as I love you.'

'Not a chance,' said his daughter.

'See you tomorrow.' And he hung up.

The accountant sat on his bed and looked at his life in a hotel room. He thought of growing older and of figures and statistics and tight butts and happy men who were fools but were loved and were good friends. And of being scared and of going home and of beautiful weekends and things not being what they seem. And of his daughter and of youth and life. Of kindness, random acts of kindness.

He looked at the snow dome.

The accountant reached for the room phone and asked for reception.

• •

He waited for the lift doors to open. He hoped he would be in time. He had felt foolish asking the moustache over the phone if the young man with the platinum hair was still in the lobby.

The doors opened and the accountant could see that the young man was picking up his rainbow bag and was heading off in the direction of the train station.

The accountant walked over to him as quickly as he could without running.

'Excuse me,' he said and the young man turned.

The accountant had no idea what to say. The two men looked at each other.

'Yes?' said the young man with the platinum hair.

The accountant held out the box to him. 'Look, I just thought you might like this, to remind you of... I just thought you might like this.'

The young man put down his rainbow bag and picked up the snow dome. He looked at the accountant and smiled the most beautiful smile.

'It's good you had a beautiful weekend,' said the accountant. 'Have a safe trip home.'

The young man with the platinum hair and rainbow bag and giant snow dome of Sydney nodded and moved off.

The accountant walked out through the glass doors and looked at the night. It was noisy and a bit smelly, but he felt a little better. He was going home tomorrow.

Across the street was a newsagency. He thought for a moment and then decided to go and buy a lottery ticket.

And he knew as he crossed the street he would never even check to see if it won. He'd just keep it in his wallet.

4

Elizabeth's News

Monica McInerney

Elizabeth liked to give herself plenty of time to write her Christmas letter. One year she'd left it until late November and had been very unhappy with the result. It had been her shortest letter ever, and, in her opinion, the most boring. The following year she opened a new file on her computer in the first week of January and from then on added a paragraph or two each month. By the time December came, all she'd needed to do was tidy up the spelling and punctuation and there it was, a twelve-part summary of her year. Since then, her letter had never dropped below six pages long.

She'd got the idea from a radio program. The announcer had been poking fun at the whole idea of people sending out a yearly round-up of their lives tucked inside Christmas cards. He'd asked listeners to call in with the more ridiculous examples of letters they had received from friends or acquaintances. There was a great flock of these letters winging around the world each year, apparently, filled with the large and small detail that made up people's lives. Renovations that had turned families upside down. Details of birthday celebrations and holidays and baby news and engagement news. People living their lives and sharing their stories with other people, friends and near-strangers alike.

The radio announcer read out a selection, putting on funny voices for the different letters and interspersing them with sarcastic remarks. But Elizabeth hadn't found any of the snippets ridiculous. She'd wanted to hear more. What had happened to the twin boys who had somehow managed to get exactly the same mark for each subject in their end-of-year exams? Did the young couple ever get their bathroom renovated, after all the disasters with the six – six, imagine – different builders they'd employed? How did that lucky grandmother manage to keep track of all those grandchildren – forty-one of them! Elizabeth had thought about those letters and their authors all afternoon. What would she put in her Christmas letter if she was to write one? She'd sat down at her computer that same afternoon to find out.

This year marked the seventh anniversary of her Christmas letter. The number of pages and the size of the mailing list had grown each year. She'd started putting all her spare change in a specially marked moneybox on top of the fridge to pay for the end-of-year postage and printing.

Her sister, Louise, was disgusted. Not at the length of the letter, or the cost of the postage, but at the 'conceit of the whole enterprise'. At the 'assumption' that 'near-strangers' would even care – or 'give a rat's', as she indelicately put it – about Elizabeth's activities during the year. Louise nearly had 'conniptions', as she also liked to say, when Elizabeth accidentally let slip during one of their rare phone conversations that there were now more than two hundred people on her mailing list.

'Two hundred! You don't even have four friends, let alone two hundred. Who on earth are you sending it to? Everyone on the electoral roll?'

As it happened, Elizabeth did have four friends, and yes, she'd had to resort to the electoral roll to confirm some of her recipients' addresses, but, the truth was, she'd had dealings with all of the people on her list. She told Louise as much.

'Dealings? What on earth does "dealings" mean?'

Elizabeth decided it was time to pretend there was someone at the door. She said a hurried farewell. 'Yes, Louise, *dealings*,' she continued aloud to herself as she walked through to her small home office. 'Contacts. Connections. Communications. Is that enough or shall I get the thesaurus?'

She was always much fiercer and more articulate in pretend conversations with her sister than in real ones. She kicked herself mentally for having made the mistake of even mentioning the Christmas letter to her. Not that Louise's scornful reaction had come as a surprise.

Elizabeth had spent nearly every year of her sixty-two years trying to negotiate the minefield of her relationship with her older sister.

Her latest letter was nearly finished. She'd experimented with both font size and layout, and was very pleased with the result. She'd found so much to write about this year. There'd also been some excellent additions to her mailing list, one as recently as that morning, after the postman had delivered three envelopes: a bill, a letter from a friend – yes, one of the four that Louise had so sneeringly referred to – and a flyer from a campaigning local politician.

Elizabeth had gone straight to her computer, opened her Christmas Mailing List file and entered in the new name and address details, carefully checking the spelling from the bottom of the politician's flyer. In just over a month's time, Rebecca Kilakos of the local branch of the Labor Party would receive Elizabeth's latest Christmas letter. So would twelve other politicians who had letter-dropped her over the past seven years; the manager of the local plumbing company; the publicity officer of the state theatre company; four funeral directors; two roofing contractors; the owners of six local takeaway businesses; the principals of the local primary school and high school; and the fundraising manager for the nearby kindergarten. Her doctor, dentist, podiatrist and chiropractor. The director of the Australian Tax Office. The CEO of Telstra. The head of Centrelink. Every person, in fact, who had ever put their name to a leaflet, letter or bill sent to Elizabeth's address.

Her letter didn't stay only in Australia. Her World Vision–sponsored child in Mozambique received it. So did the President of Ireland. Elizabeth had read about her in a guide book in her local library and liked the simplicity of the address: The President of Ireland, Phoenix Park, Dublin, Ireland. After that, it only seemed fair to add the Prime Minister of Australia and the Queen of England, not to mention all the other Royals, Presidents and heads of state around the world. Elizabeth liked imagining her Christmas letter arriving in grand offices in Canberra, London, Washington, Copenhagen, Montreal, Paris, Tokyo. She sent it to her favourite opera singers, well-known sports stars, Oscar-winning actors, Booker Prize–winning authors and ground-breaking scientists. Anyone who caught her attention and whose address – or the address of their managers, agents, publishers or record companies – was easy to find.

She enjoyed looking over the mix of names and addresses as she peeled off the labels and fixed them to her envelopes. It was quite a project these days, printing, collating and folding all those letters, stuffing more than two hundred envelopes, sticking on all those stamps, but many years of secretarial work had given her all the skills she needed. She always made an occasion of it. She'd take her time getting everything organised on her dining room table, play Christmas music, even turn on the lights of her small Christmas tree for the whole day, not just after dark as she usually did to keep her electricity costs down.

Sometimes Louise's voice would get into her head, in the early stages of the envelope labelling at least. Not that Louise knew Elizabeth was still sending out a letter each year. The scornful phone call had taken place three years previously, and Elizabeth always made sure Louise and her family weren't accidentally added to the mailing list. She could just imagine what Louise would say about it if she did receive a copy.

Elizabeth's solution when Louise's voice came into her head was to turn the Christmas carols up louder. She'd get into a lovely rhythm with her letter folding, envelope stuffing, labelling and stamping and, before too long, her table would be covered with neat piles of envelopes, all sorted into countries to make it easier for the people in the post office.

For her, the pleasure was all in the writing and sending out of the letter each year. It had been an unexpected but pleasing bonus when some recipients started writing back. She'd received a form card from the Queen of Denmark one year, and a signed photograph of an ageing American actor the next. *Dear Elizabeth, Wishing you and your family a happy year ahead*, read another one of the cards – a mass-printed, not handwritten, one from a federal politician. Family? She had no family. Apart from Louise, of course, but she lived on the other side of the country and they barely spoke. Elizabeth liked the sound of it, though. *You and your family.*

It was so easy the next time she sat down to do her Christmas letter to include some information about her 'family'. An ordinary family, she decided. A family anyone who read her Christmas letter could relate to. She'd barely had to think about it before the words appeared on the screen in front of her.

> In family news, it's been an even busier year than normal. Mel, my husband, [Elizabeth named him after the Melway street directory on the shelf in front of her.] has done a wonderful job renovating the bathroom. The girls are loving high school. [*What to call them?* Elizabeth wondered. She looked out her window to her neighbour's garden.] Iris is thinking of going on to become a teacher, while Rose says she is happy to live one day at a time and enjoy her final schooldays while she can. 'Life's too short not to have fun, Mum,' she said to me last week. Out of the mouths of babes!

It was that simple. With a touch of the computer keys she'd given herself a handyman husband and two teenage daughters. And so what if their ages didn't quite tally with her own. She'd never mentioned how old she was, in any case.

The letter writing became even more of a treat than before. She kept to her schedule, one entry each month.

The thinking time in between entries became as enjoyable as the writing. She discovered there were no limits to what she could write about. There was no one telling her to stick to the facts, after all. It wasn't as if she was a court reporter, or a journalist, was it? It wasn't as if the Queen or the President of the United States or even the fundraiser from her local kindergarten was going to ring her up with a few queries.

In her next entry she gave herself an interesting job at a local school. She extended her house. She gave herself a car, a five-year-old Toyota Corolla that 'we have nicknamed Skippy on account of the embarrassing kangaroo hops it likes to do at traffic lights'. She wrote in enthusiastic terms about her plans for a garden. The reality – an enclosed concrete yard at the back of her apartment – faded as she worked from a colourful garden magazine beside her.

> Mel and I decided to try and be as self-sufficient as possible this year. It was a sacrifice, but I agreed to give up half of my flower garden for a vegetable patch. We decided we'd do it as a trial run. So far we've planted lettuces, tomatoes, corn and spring onions. If I can just keep the snails and the birds away, we're in for a very healthy summer of food!

Inspiration seemed to come from everywhere. On the way home from her weekly trip to the local supermarket, she'd jumped at the sudden sound of an ambulance siren behind her. The driver had obviously just got a call. She watched as the ambulance screeched to a halt, did a rapid U-turn and went at lawbreaking speed in the opposite direction.

Once she arrived home, Elizabeth went straight to the computer, without unpacking her groceries.

Amid all the good times, we had our fair share of drama this year. The first incident was in March, when I was called out of work [She needed to check back through the previous entries to remember where she said she was working. A local secondary school, she discovered, as the Classics teacher. She deleted the word 'work'.] called out of the classroom to take an urgent call from Mel. Iris had been knocked off her bike on the way to her part-time job. I'm sure all the parents among you can imagine how I felt at that moment. Mel hastily assured me she was fine, just a broken ankle, no head injuries, but I will never forget that terrible moment. Does every mother fear the worst for her children? I nearly made it to the hospital before the ambulance, I drove so fast, but fortunately Iris truly was all right. Shocked, bruised and with some nasty looking scrapes, but as we all said many times over the next month or two, it could have been so much worse.

Elizabeth's second daughter also found herself in hospital that year.

It seems accidents in our family were contagious this year. Barely was Iris back on her two feet than Rose found herself in the accident and emergency ward of our local hospital!

Elizabeth stopped there. What could have happened to Rose? Had she stayed in hospital for long? Was it a nice hospital? Elizabeth was blessed with good health and had never actually spent even so much as a night in hospital. It seemed too important a place to make a mistake about, details-wise. She saved the document, turned off the computer, locked up the house and set off at a fast walk to her nearest tram stop.

Four hours later she not only had excellent first-hand details of the interior of her local hospital and a list of Rose's possible accidents and resulting injuries, she also had another five names to add to her mailing list: the CEO of the hospital, the head nursing sister, the maintenance manager, the midwife and the gardener.

It had been a lovely afternoon. She'd gone into the waiting room of the outpatients department and, literally, waited. It was much better than sitting in a coffee shop, or wandering in her local shopping centre, the way she'd been spending her days since she retired. In those places it was often quite hard to strike up conversations with people. Here in the waiting room it seemed everyone wanted to talk. It was the adrenalin, Elizabeth supposed. The shock. The relief of being in a hospital after the excitement or scare of whatever had got them there in the first place.

She spoke to fifteen different people. They were all so friendly. A young woman with a little baby who had nearly choked on a marble. A middle-aged man who'd badly cut his finger while pruning his apple tree. A teenage boy covered in red spots. If anyone asked why she was there, she made a vague gesture toward her stomach. 'Women's troubles?' an elderly woman (who had tripped over her garden hose and was waiting to have her ankle seen to) whispered. Elizabeth nodded. The elderly woman patted her on the hand. Elizabeth was shocked to feel the tears well. It was the first physical contact she'd had in months. Perhaps even years.

Back home, in front of the computer, she'd opened the file for her Christmas letter and typed as rapidly as she could. Within a few sentences she'd almost convinced herself that her youngest daughter really had nearly come to a sticky end, after a freak accident involving a bicycle, a local plumber and an unsecured ladder.

Onlookers told Mel and I that it was like something from a Laurel and Hardy film, with buckets clanging and ladders swinging, and poor Rose's bike somehow caught up in one of the rungs being pulled behind the van. Funny in retrospect, yes, but it wasn't funny at the time, let me tell you! Rose was lucky to get away with just a dislocated shoulder and a rather nasty cut on her right side that required more than fifteen stitches. Of course, every cloud has a silver lining – I'm happy to report that romance blossomed for Rose in the emergency ward! She was in a cubicle beside a lovely young man called Shane, an apprentice electrician, who'd come a cropper after getting an electric shock while up on the roof of a house he was rewiring. As Shane said, sparks really flew that day, in more ways than one! It's early days, of course, they are both still so young, but Mel and I are agreed that they make a lovely couple.

In her yearly letters since then, Shane and Rose's relationship had gone from strength to strength. Elizabeth had shared the happy news of their engagement, the joyful day of their marriage and the even more wonderful day, ten months later, when Rose had given birth to twins, 'a beautiful boy called Alexander who is the absolute spit of his grandfather' and 'the sweetest little girl they've named Bethany and, yes, the Beth is after me!'

Her letters weren't always about the children. She'd decided to give Mel early retirement, and had resigned from her teaching job too. 'It's given us both the most amazing new lease of life! We've decided life is for living and that age is going to be no barrier for us!'

She gave them both a rail holiday through Europe. She'd never been outside Australia herself, but it amazed her how much information she was able to find on the internet and in her local library.

For any of you who have read *Murder on the Orient Express* or seen the film, I'm happy to report that the real thing is even better than you could imagine. Oh, the luxury! I felt like the Queen of Sheba, the Queen of England and the Queen of All She Surveys rolled into one. Mel found it all very funny, teasing me that I started the trip speaking in my normal voice and finished it sounding as though I had a mouth full of plums!

The following year, she and Mel took a cruise through the Mediterranean. Elizabeth visited more than a dozen travel agents around the city, gathering brochures and asking questions.

> It truly was a floating hotel. We almost forgot we were on the ocean sometimes. We'd heard horror stories of mass outbreaks of food poisoning, even attacks by pi-rates – and of course there's no forgetting the threat of an iceberg à la the Titanic, is there?! – but thankfully our journey was event-free. Mel's begged me not to tell you all about his early landlubber days, but I just can't resist. I had never imagined having a green husband, but it's true, seasickness does bring the most amazing green shade to one's skin. Thankfully he gained his sea legs after a few days and was soon playing quoits, swimming and social-ising with the best of them.

There was nothing she and Mel wouldn't try. She learned guitar one year. Mel took up Morris dancing. They both tried karate. Mel learned to waterski. They joined the local amateur dramatic society, landing lead roles in a well-reviewed production of Muriel Sparks's *The Prime of Miss Jean Brodie*. What with all their extra-curricular activities, not to mention the regular family dinners and babysitting duties – her other daughter, Iris, had also had a child: 'sadly, she and the father are no longer a couple but thankfully they have both decided their daughter Lily's welfare comes first and they are wonderful parents' – they barely had a moment to themselves.

This year's letter was Elizabeth's most action-packed yet. To her own astonishment, she'd climbed Mount Kilimanjaro. Not to the highest peak – she decided to show some restraint – but to a lower, more accessible point, still nearly four thousand metres above sea level.

> Yes, at my age! I've been secretly preparing for it for the past two years, getting fit, lifting weights, beginning with long hikes. My doctor nearly had kittens when I told him what I was planning, but to his credit he soon got behind me and helped me develop a realistic training plan. Mel has been wonderful, as always. I think he was worried I'd taken on too much, but as he said, 'There's no-one like you when it comes to determination, Lizzy. If anyone can do it, you can!'

As always, she began printing the year's letters and address labels on 5 December. The final few of the three hundred labels – a personal best, numbers-wise – had just emerged from the printer when her phone rang. The sudden sound made her jump. Her phone didn't ring very often.

It was her sister, Louise. Elizabeth hadn't heard from her in many weeks. As usual, there were no polite pleasantries. She was coming to Melbourne in the New Year, Louise explained briskly to Elizabeth. Her husband had a work trip and Louise had decided to join him and do some shopping in the January sales at the same time.

Before Elizabeth had a chance to offer an invitation, Louise turned it down. 'We won't stay with you. Dennis's company is putting us up in a very nice hotel. I've a long list of sales I want to go to but I'll try and drop out to you on the last afternoon.'

It was hard not to be hurt at the words 'try' and 'last afternoon', as if Elizabeth was so far down Louise's list of priorities that the visit wasn't a certainty and she would leave it to the end of her trip, rather than come there as soon as she could.

'That's fine,' Elizabeth said into the phone, pushing the hurt feeling down as far as she could.

Louise picked up something in her voice. 'What is it? What's wrong?'

'Nothing,' Elizabeth said.

'It's a work trip for Dennis. I'll need to be on hand for him, but I'll drop out to you. No need to be snippy. It's not as if you are rushing over to see us all the time. How long is it since you've been home? Five years? More?'

Seven years, five months and thirteen days. Elizabeth never had any trouble remembering the date she left Perth for Melbourne. She didn't correct Louise. It would only annoy her. As much and as often as Elizabeth tried to behave differently, she'd always annoyed Louise one way or another, throughout their lives.

'She's jealous of you,' Elizabeth's grandmother had said once. Even fifty-two years later, Elizabeth hadn't forgotten the conversation or the incident that preceded it. A row over a board game that turned into a spat that developed into a nasty fight that resulted in a large hank of the ten-year-old Elizabeth's hair ending up in the sixteen-year-old Louise's fist. It had taken Elizabeth several months to grow back enough hair to cover the bald spot.

Elizabeth had tried to understand her grandmother's words, but failed. 'How can she be jealous of me? She was here first. She's got everything.' Elizabeth truly believed that. Louise was tall, whereas Elizabeth had inherited her mother's petite build. Louise had lovely flowing black hair, whereas Elizabeth had a tangle of mousy-coloured curls. Louise could play the piano beautifully. Elizabeth barely managed to make a squawking noise on her recorder.

Her grandmother had smoothed back Elizabeth's curls and gently kissed the spot that still hurt, even hours after Louise had done her tugging. 'It's because she was here first that she's jealous of you, Lizzy. You took the attention away from her. I told your mother she was spoiling Louise too much, that she was making it very hard for herself and whichever child might arrive next, but she didn't listen. She treated her so much like a little princess that your sister believes she is a little princess. And through no fault of your own, you arrived and became a trespasser. You stepped on her patch.'

'But what can I do about it? It's not my fault, is it?'

'Of course it's not your fault. I'm just telling you so you understand. It will seem impossible at times but you have to try and ignore it. Try and feel sorry for her if you can.'

Sometimes feeling sorry for her worked, but mostly it didn't. It seemed that anything Elizabeth did drove Louise into either a fit of anger, or derision, or tears. As she moved from childhood into teenage years, Elizabeth learned the best way to keep the peace in their house was to do as little, and stay as quiet, as possible. If she did manage to do something, she said as little as possible about it, to her parents but also, and especially, to Louise.

It became second nature to her. She kept quiet about the good results she got in her secretarial exams, mindful that Louise had failed hers six years previously. She only casually mentioned the job offers she received after sending her CV to every business in their area. Louise had been offered a job in a local real estate office only after their father had personally approached every member of his Rotary Club. Elizabeth sat back as Louise commandeered the dinner table night after night and told their parents every detail about her job, about the parties she was going to, all the friends she had. Elizabeth kept quiet as Louise announced that one of the junior partners in the office had asked her out. She managed to smile when Louise announced her engagement and then in the next breath said, without looking at Elizabeth, that she had decided to ask her three best friends to be her bridesmaids. 'We're all the same height so it will look better for the photos. Would you like to be an usher, Elizabeth?'

As it happened, Elizabeth was much happier as an usher than a bridesmaid. She'd never looked good in the pale blue colour that Louise chose for her bridesmaids' dresses. It was much more fun to be greeting people at the back of the church than trying to calm Louise's nerves back in the house. She had noticed within moments of the bridal party arriving that Louise's bridesmaids each wore a fraught expression.

If she'd been bridesmaid rather than usher, she also wouldn't have fallen into conversation with the young man in the ill-fitting suit who'd been hired to drive the bridal limousine. If she'd been up at the altar, tugging at her tight blue satin dress like the other bridesmaids, she wouldn't have noticed what kind eyes the driver had. She wouldn't have had a chance to hear his funny stories about other driving jobs, or learnt that he was only driving cars to make money while he saved up for his own car-hire business. She would not have learnt that his name was Thomas. She most definitely wouldn't have had the opportunity to accept when he invited her to meet him again the following weekend.

Louise took all the credit, of course. Elizabeth let her. It was easier. She stayed quiet at all family outings, even at her own engagement party twelve months later, when Louise insisted on telling everyone the story of the happy couple's meeting, and how, if it wasn't for her wedding day, they would never have met, let alone started working together in his new business, let alone ended up marrying each other. Elizabeth had told Thomas everything about Louise, including what her grandmother had said about her being jealous. Thomas had soon learnt to stay quiet when Louise was around too.

It suited Elizabeth and Thomas to keep their news to themselves. They liked their privacy. They liked going back home to their own small house and shutting the world, and especially Louise, out. Not completely. Elizabeth loved her parents enough not to cut herself away from them. But as the years went by, and each family occasion turned into a Latest News from Louise event, she and Thomas drew further away. They made their own life. They took regular holidays, heading away in an old caravan they had bought and renovated themselves. They held dinner parties for close friends, Thomas always the cook – he was much better in the kitchen than Elizabeth. They also laughed a lot together. Thomas's sense of humour and eye for detail made him a wonderful storyteller.

Elizabeth knew there was gossip about them. Was it healthy for a husband and wife to spend so much time together, at work and at home? What about children? Didn't they want any, or weren't they able to have them?

Had they been to the doctor about it? What about adoption? As Louise effortlessly produced four children – two boys, two girls, at exactly two years apart – Elizabeth and Thomas stayed quiet. Any crying they did – and they did plenty – they did at home, together.

Once, Elizabeth overheard her nieces discussing her at one of Louise's extravagant wedding anniversary parties. 'Do you suppose Mum got all Aunty Elizabeth's share of words too? You never hear a peep out of her when Mum's around.'

'You never hear a peep out of any of us when Mum's around,' the other niece had said dolefully.

'Timid', Louise's husband had once called Elizabeth. 'Miss Meek and Mild'. He'd been drunk at the time. Elizabeth had remembered her grandmother's advice, for the thousandth time, and said nothing. She was neither timid, nor mild, nor meek. She just didn't always feel like talking, especially when Louise was in earshot.

When her elderly parents died within two months of each other, her mother from cancer, her father of a heart attack, Elizabeth watched as Louise stepped into the role of chief mourner and grieving daughter. She recalled her grandmother's words as Louise insisted on delivering the eulogy at each funeral service. There was plenty Elizabeth could have said, and plenty she did say when there was just Thomas to listen, but, in public at least, she kept her thoughts to herself.

Until the day Thomas was killed in a car accident, one week before they were due to celebrate their thirtieth wedding anniversary. That changed everything. There weren't enough hours in the day for her to say all she needed to say. She couldn't keep quiet. It came spilling and welling and rushing out of her: the anger, the unfairness, the grief, the missing, the longing, the horrible aching pain of it. She couldn't stop talking about Thomas, about his life, their life, going over every detail as if to imprint it all in her mind, before it was too late and the tiniest snippet was forgotten. She couldn't stop crying. Their house, once her refuge, gave her no peace or sanctuary. It hurt to be there when Thomas wasn't. She became restless. She felt like a pinball in a machine lurching from one place to another, ending up each time, inexplicably, at her sister's house.

For the first time in her life she asked her sister for help. She asked her sister to listen.

Perhaps Louise did at first, in the raw early days and weeks. Elizabeth's memory of that time was so fogged she couldn't remember if Louise had paid her any attention, if she had even been in the room with her.

But there was no mistaking the day Louise's patience ran out. It was a summer morning. They were sitting in Louise's kitchen. Elizabeth had received a letter from the insurance company querying an aspect of Thomas's policy and any calm she'd started to feel had shattered. She'd caught a bus directly to Louise's house. She didn't realise she was crying until Louise's words, the impatient look on her face, the tone in her voice, started to register.

'It's just a form letter, Elizabeth. You're overreacting. You have to pull yourself together. It's been four months since the accident and you're still a mess. People are starting to talk about you.'

'Talk about me?'

'You must realise what you've been like. Crying at the drop of a hat. The girls said their friends saw you walking in the park talking to yourself. It's not normal, Elizabeth, you know that. And, quite honestly, I haven't got any more time to spare listening to all of this stuff.'

'This *stuff*?' Elizabeth said in a cold voice that surprised herself.

There was no buffer between them now. She couldn't glance across at Thomas to keep her temper calm. There wasn't the knowledge that when they left and got into their car to drive home, they'd be able to talk and laugh about Louise and her selfish ways. There was no car anymore. It had been so badly damaged in the accident that took Thomas's life that Elizabeth not only didn't want to see it again, she hadn't been able to get into any car since. She had tried once and all she could think about were the last moments of Thomas's life, the truck sliding and screeching towards his car, him being trapped in that tangled mess of steel, while just a few kilometres away she was at home, in the kitchen, oblivious, expecting the sound of his key in the front door.

'And you need to get yourself another car,' Louise was saying. 'How are you going to get around without one, for heaven's sake?'

The answer came to Elizabeth in a flash of clarity. 'I'll take public transport.'

Louise made a sniffing sound. 'Public transport? There are three buses a day around here if you're lucky.'

'I'll take the tram.'

Louise looked at her as if she had lost all reason. 'There are no trams in Perth, Elizabeth.'

'I'm not staying here. I'm moving to Melbourne.'

'Melbourne? *Melbourne*? Why on earth would you go and live in — '

Elizabeth blocked out the rest of Louise's words that morning and in the days afterwards. She sold the business she and Thomas had built from scratch, the house they had lived in for so many years. She was packed and gone within three weeks.

Looking back, she didn't know if her sudden move across the country made the months that followed easier or harder. Each day would have brought pain and sorrow and anger, regardless of where she was, she felt sure.

One of the first things she installed after buying her small apartment in an eastern suburb of Melbourne was an answering machine. It helped sometimes to hide behind it. Louise treated it as a personal recording studio, leaving long messages once a fortnight, filling Elizabeth in on her family's latest achievements, before ending each call with a pause, then a clipped 'Well, Elizabeth, I hope you're feeling better'. Elizabeth picked up the phone occasionally and had a brief conversation, but the habit of too many years proved hard to break. She returned to being silent in Louise's company, keeping her thoughts to herself again.

Almost to herself. Three months after she arrived in Melbourne she went to see someone. A professional. Louise had left a message on her machine saying she thought Elizabeth had developed a mental illness. That she had become 'deranged with grief'. It wasn't normal to 'cut yourself off from everyone like this'. It wasn't 'natural' to be so sad for so long.

Elizabeth agreed with Louise. She did feel deranged. Unhinged. Rearranged. She felt she had been torn apart the moment the policeman came to the door and told her Thomas was dead. That the pieces still hadn't come back together properly.

She was wrong, the professional told her. If anything, Elizabeth was grieving perfectly. 'You loved him, he died suddenly, you are mourning him with every fibre of yourself,' the woman said.

That was it. That was exactly it, Elizabeth realised. Every fibre, every muscle, every cell of her body was missing Thomas. Missing what they had had together, what they had planned to do together, missing all the moments they would have shared together.

'There's nothing wrong with you, Elizabeth,' the professional said at their final appointment. 'Thomas was a lucky man to have been loved so much. Be true to your feelings. Grieve as you want to. Talk about him. Write letters about him. Shout. Dance. Sing. It's your grief, your feelings, your life. You live it the way you want to.'

The woman's words were like a war cry to Elizabeth. She felt she'd been given permission to be herself.

She started slowly. If she woke in the morning and didn't feel like seeing anyone that day, she didn't. If she woke feeling brighter, then she would venture into the nearest shopping centre, browse a little, chat to the assistants, until the peace of her little flat called her back. She started listening to the radio, all day long enjoying the hum of voices in the background, the bite-sized doses of current affairs, the debates and the interviews.

She started to write letters. A radio program put the idea into her head. She'd been sitting in her small living room, gazing out the window, when the presenter caught her attention with a mock-dramatic speech. 'I am sad to announce the death of the letter,' he said in a voice akin to wartime declarations. A lively phone-in followed, older listeners bemoaning the lack of personal correspondence, the end of the days of thank you letters, get well notes and news-filled aerograms. Younger listeners defended the speed and convenience of emails and texts. The announcer finished the segment in a joking tone. 'Fight back, everyone. Pick up those pens, shake out that paper. Your post office needs you.'

During her next visit to the local shopping centre, Elizabeth bought a stationery set. The young woman who served her was so nice, so friendly, so patient that Elizabeth asked for her name. At home that afternoon, she took out a sheet of paper and wrote a polite note to the manager of the stationery shop, praising his young assistant and complimenting him on the splendid range of stationery he stocked. Two days later she received a letter back. 'Your note made our day. Thank you for taking the time to write.'

The following week she wrote to her local post office to thank them for their punctual deliveries, day after day, good weather or bad. It amused her when she didn't hear back. Perhaps her letter had gone missing in the post. She wrote to the manager of the local coffee shop to say thank you after receiving an extra chocolate with her weekly cappuccino. She wrote to the manager of the parks and garden section of her council to compliment them on the beautiful display of spring flowers in front of the municipal offices. She kept copies of all the letters she sent out, and attached any replies. Within three months she had a drawer filled with correspondence.

The Christmas letters seemed a natural progression. She'd bought a computer by that stage. Her first letter had been a tentative affair, less than a page. She'd sent it to only five people. The list hadn't included Louise. The following year it ran to two pages, but she still hadn't felt satisfied. The third year she invented Mel and Rose and Iris. They'd starred in her letters ever since. It didn't feel at all disloyal to Thomas. On the contrary, she suspected he would have approved. He'd liked keeping their own lives to themselves as much as she had. She'd had no trouble with material since. If anything, it had been hard to keep her imagination in check, and the letters under twelve pages long.

Oh, she knew it was odd to be sending these imaginary life stories out to complete strangers, but the truth of it was she was having fun. Fun. She was enjoying herself. It wasn't any attempt to invent a fake life to cover over her sad, pitiful existence. That wasn't how she felt about her life anymore. She would always be sad at the thought of Thomas's early death, at all they had missed out on together, but that terrible time was part of her now, inside her body, in her skin, not some monster that ruled over her. Memories of him gave her solace and pleasure now, not a rush of anger or hurt or fear or terror.

She wasn't lonely, either. She had all the friends she needed. Four. One travelled often and sent her amusing, interesting postcards each time. One lived down the road and her door was always open to Elizabeth, she'd made that clear. The other two were back in Western Australia and each visited once a year, for a week apiece. Letters kept the connection strong in between times.

Nor was she bored. For the past four years, she'd worked as a volunteer at the local hospital. The afternoon doing research for Rose's accident had given her the idea. Twice a week she spent the day in the waiting room, offering tea, a listening ear, the touch of a hand.

'Are you a religious nut?' one of the waiting patients asked her once. Another had sniffed suspiciously at the cup of tea Elizabeth offered him, as though it might be poisoned. One woman had almost snarled at her, telling her to go away. But most people appreciated her. They'd talk, a little or a lot. They'd gratefully accept the tea. They'd take one of the magazines she offered. Sometimes she just sat in silence beside them. 'Does the hospital pay you to do this?' she was asked once. No, she'd answered. 'Well, they should.'

The week before Christmas, she'd just arrived home from her hospital visit and picked up a satisfying pile of cards from the mat, when she noticed the light flashing on her answering machine. Ten missed calls. Before she had a chance to play them, the phone rang. She'd barely said hello before her sister's voice rushed down the line to her.

'Have you completely lost your mind?'

'Hello, Louise. Yes, I'm well, thanks. And you? And the family?'

Louise ignored her. 'You promised me you'd stop. You didn't, did you? This has been going on for *years*, hasn't it?'

'Stop what?'

'These ridiculous Christmas letters. Can you even imagine how embarrassing it was for me? Standing in the middle of the supermarket and hearing your nonsense broadcast over the entire shopping centre.'

'Pardon me?'

'He read them out, Elizabeth. The man at the radio station read your letters out.' Louise said the words as though she was speaking to a very small, very stupid child.

'How did you know they were my letters?'

'Your name, Elizabeth. Your own name. In full. Couldn't you at least have written them under a pseudonym? But no, you didn't think of me, did you? You didn't imagine that they would fall into the hands of a radio announcer who would think it was funny to read them all aloud, and make a joke of you, did you?'

'Yes, I did, actually.'

'He was poking fun at you, Elizabeth. You should have heard the voices he used, the – What did you say?'

'I said, of course I imagined them being read out. That's why I sent them.' She'd posted them to dozens of radio announcers around the country. It had been so easy to find their names and addresses on the internet. She'd not only sent her most recent letter, but copies of all her letters from the past seven years. They'd made quite a bulky parcel.

'*You* sent them? You?'

'They asked people to do it.' She'd heard it on one of the late-night national programs. 'It's that time of year again, folks,' the smiling-voiced man had said. 'Christmas letter time. Have you had any yet? Written any yourself? Don't just share your news with your friends and family. Share it with the entire nation.' Elizabeth had secretly hoped one of her recipients would ring in and read out snippets from her letters and had been unaccountably disappointed when they didn't.

Louise was speechless for only a few seconds. 'He devoted a whole segment to you, do you realise that? How could you embarrass me like this? Embarrass everyone that might know me? Embarrass yourself, more to the point, with this, I don't know what to call it, this manifesto of madness?'

Elizabeth had to stop herself laughing out loud. She made a note of the term on the pad beside the phone: 'manifesto of madness'. Thomas would have liked that too.

'You know this isn't normal behaviour, don't you? You know you don't really have a husband? Two daughters? That you're not a Classics teacher? That you haven't just climbed Mount *Kilimanjaro*? Have you flipped your lid again?'

Elizabeth made a note of the phrase 'flipped your lid' on the notepad in front of her too. She kept her voice calm. 'No, Louise, I'm quite sane, I promise you. I know that none of that is true. I am fully aware of the fact that in my real life I'm a childless stay-at-home widow.'

'Then what on earth are you doing?'

Elizabeth could have explained. She could have talked about the power of imagination, about having fun, about not doing anyone any harm with her letters. If anything, people were possibly enjoying them. Of course she could have told the truth in her letters, but where was the fun in that, for herself or her readers, or even the radio listeners?

Louise was still ranting down the phone line. 'What's it all about this time, Elizabeth? Another desperate cry for attention?'

Once again, Elizabeth could have tried to explain. Once again, Louise didn't give her the opportunity.

'And you don't even write "Happy Christmas" at the end,' her sister continued. 'You sign it "With all best wishes", as if it had nothing to do with Christmas at all. If you're going to do something this ridiculous, couldn't you at least do it properly?'

Louise was right. Elizabeth had never signed off her letters with 'Happy Christmas'. She preferred the look of 'With all best wishes'. That way the wishes covered the whole year ahead, too, not just one day in December.

If she was going to wish someone a Happy Christmas, she preferred to do it in person.

'What will people think, Elizabeth? That your life is so empty, so meaningless, you have to concoct complete fantasies to —'

As her sister continued to berate her, Elizabeth stepped back from the phone table, looking into her lounge room. It looked so cheerful with its Christmas decorations, the small tree adorned in lights, its main wall covered in photos of her and Thomas.

There was no point in trying to explain her newly rebuilt life to Louise. There never had been. Louise only ever saw what she wanted to see. She only ever heard what she wanted to hear. For a moment Elizabeth imagined Thomas across the room from her, the amused expression he would wear whenever Elizabeth was on the phone to Louise, as the one-sided conversation went on and on, the way he would say afterwards, 'You have the patience of a saint, my Lizzy'.

Elizabeth decided it was only right to end the call, as soon as possible, in the spirit of the season.

'Happy Christmas, Louise,' she said.

And then, very gently and for the first time in her life, she hung up on her sister.

5

Ithaca in My Mind

Peter Temple

From the terrace, the eye was led down the thin lap pool edged with Castlemaine bluestone pavers and flanked by box hedges to the stone bench in front of the ivy-clad brick wall.

Vincent Duncan was sitting in a cane chair, naked beneath a blue towelling dressing-gown, a telephone in his left hand. With his right hand, he was toying with grey hairs on his chest.

'Sorry, say that again,' he said.

'Carter wants to pass.'

'Pass what?'

Duncan pulled a hair. It hurt in a pleasant way. He studied the tiny pale root that had lived in his flesh. What did hairs feed on?

'He doesn't want it,' said Marjorie.

She had the voice of an upper-class English twelve-year-old. That was in part understandable because she had once been an upper-class English twelve-year-old.

She lived in London with a man called Rufus, who had certainly once been an undersized twelve-year-old. Now he had a moustache like Neville Chamberlain and wrote oversized accounts of British military disasters involving acts of heroic selflessness, mainly by the officers.

Marjorie and Rufus lived in a flat in what had once been a power station. Architects were engaged to make the place even more cold and brutal. Duncan had spent a night there. It was like living in a missile silo designed by the Bauhaus.

'I don't think it's quite Carter,' said Marjorie. 'Well, it's probably not so much him as the new lot wanting to prune the mid-list.'

'The mid-list's got what to do with me, Marjorie?' he said.

'Of course it's silly judgement on their part,' she said, 'but there it is. I'm afraid you are mid-list, darling, and we probably have to live with it.'

'Marjorie,' he said, 'Carter's a stupid prick. I never liked him. Let's go elswhere.'

'Vincent,' said Marjorie, 'I've shown the book around.'

'Talked to Random?'

'I've spoken to Random, yes. Vincent, things are not what they were. Tastes change, you know that. We may have to batten down. In the long term, your . . .'

'Well, how much?'

'It's not actually about the money.'

'It never is. Random. They're offering what?'

'Random passed on it too.'

Duncan felt the cobweb tingle of pain across his scalp. It was cold. He pulled at the dressing gown to close it and saw the veins on his feet. Since when had they been big, so grotesque, that revolting colour?

'Well, stuff Random too,' he said. 'Stuff Bertelsmann, stuff the Germans. Let's go to Revanche. He wants me, that pretty boy.'

Majorie made a throaty sound. 'To simply say it, Vincent, I've walked both sides of the steet. I've been offered five thousand pounds by Flashman and it is the only offer and I'm not sure how long it's open.'

'Ludicrous,' Duncan said. 'Insulting.'

'You mustn't take it personally. That is really important.'

'Marjorie,' he said, 'I take it very personally. I cannot tell you how important this book is to me. I am in a position where if . . .'

He took a deep breath. 'Marjorie, if this book doesn't attract the best advance of my career, I may never write another novel.'

Marjorie was talking to someone. 'Sorry, Vincent, the other line. Yes, your career. Well, it's been pretty good, hasn't it, darling. I mean, *Ithaca*, what's that added up to over the years?'

'Gus consumed the proceeds of *Ithaca*,' he said. 'The tax office and then Augustine.'

'You've insisted on marrying them, Vincent. And without pre-nups. That really is unprotected sex.'

Duncan wanted to ask the podgy parasite what she knew of pre-nups and unprotected sex. Any sex. The historian almost certainly had his saggy bottom caned elsewhere.

But he needed Marjorie as never before. He needed her even more than he needed to find Hugh Merill-Porter, formerly of Toorak, the accountant who insisted he put everything, including the house, into the share market.

'Gear,' said Hugh. 'Gear and grow very rich, Vincent. That's all I have to say. You will thank me.'

When he found Merill-Porter, believed to be in a Philippine bolthole, he would say, 'Pain, Hugh. Pain. That's all I have to say.'

Then his hired help would torture Hugh Merill-Porter. It would not bring back the one million-plus bucks lost by investing in house-of-cards property companies now insolvent. Nor would it restore ownership of the terrace. But watching it on video late at night would be satisfying.

At least he'd stopped marrying them after Gus.

'Marjorie,' Duncan said. 'I need the sort of advance I got for *The Taint of Speech*. In that vicinity. Or I may never write again.'

Shrill laughter in the background.

Was he on Marjorie's speakerphone?

She would die. He would travel to England and kill her.

'Sorry about the noise,' said Marjorie. 'It's Emily's birthday.'

And Emily too would die. Enjoy, Ems. This is your last birthday.

'The *Taint* sort of advance,' he said. 'Or I may never write again.'

A sigh.

'Darling,' said Marjorie, '*Taint* was on the back of *Ithaca*. You were hot, darling. But *Taint* tanked, there's no other way to say it. And *Rough Forked Beast* didn't find a readership either. And so we are at the point where, dare I say it, there may not be an enormous amount of pent-up expectation. Forked, really.'

She'd been drinking.

'Have they actually read the actual book?' said Duncan.

'There is no way of knowing, my dear. Short of water-boarding them.'

'But you've conveyed the, ah, essence? The man and the polar bear and the woman and the girl and the journey to the cave full of books? The . . .'

'Yes, dear. We wrote a compelling blurb. Not an easy work to encapsulate, I have to say. Em did it brilliantly. Márquez, Coetzee, McCarthy, the tiger thing.'

'Oh God no, Marjorie, not the bloody tiger?'

'With respect, Vincent, the tiger was huge. We have tried to put *A Seducing Fire* ...'

'*A Reducing Fire*, Marjorie. *Reducing*.'

'Yes. We've tried to put it in the company of hugeness. Associate it with hugeness.'

'And?'

'They didn't make any specific comments. Just said pass.'

Shrieks in the background.

'Darling,' said Marjorie. 'I'm being summoned, have to go, ring you back, not today, that's chockablock. Pecker up.'

The sudden fire in his brain.

'Marjorie,' he said, 'it occurs to me that I might need another agent. How does that sit with you, darling? You've lived a fat life off me and now you come along with this pathetic confession of inadequacy and just plain bloody stupid and hopeless ...'

Duncan thought he could hear sluglike marine creatures crawling over the cable at the bottom of the Indian Ocean.

'Thank you for making this easier, Vincent,' she said, voice of the headmistress of Malory Towers. 'I've had enough of you. I am terminating our agency agreement, backdated to before you delivered this fourth-rate piece of sentimental rubbish. You will have the email within five minutes. Goodbye.'

The connection was ended. Duncan held a piece of moulded plastic in his hand.

Haig's voice from behind him.

'Bye, be back late,' she said. 'You really should go to the gym.'

He turned, saw only a gleam of bare shoulders, hair, she was gone.

Gone.

He sat. He heard her car coming out of the garage, heard it gunned down the street, around the corner.

It was an Alfa.

'I have to have an Alfa, darling,' she had said. 'It makes me feel sexy.'

Who was the beneficiary of that? Not the mug who paid for it, paid the exhorbitant repair and service bills. He calculated that every time it went in to the dealer, he paid the weekly wage of a mechanic and two slabs of beer.

Well, it wouldn't be going in at his expense again. The letter from Stronzo Italia or whatever it was called said they'd handed him over to the lawyers.

A magpie landed beside the pool. Its first contemptuous act was to defecate. From on high, this arrogant bird had chosen his sliver of land to descend upon in order to shit on his hand-cut Castlemaine bluestone pavers.

Hand-cut. The twinky little landscape designer brought in by the skeletal architect had used the term.

Rock pavers cut by hand? Men sitting around with hammers, tapping away? Rubbish. They were cut with massive howling power saws. Kryptonite-tipped blades came down and sliced the ancient olivine basalt.

Duncan showered in the marble-floored glass box, talking to himself. 'The swine,' he said. 'The ignorant swine. They can't do this to me.'

He blow-dried his hair. He'd left it too late for plugs, that was a major regret. While you still had enough, you could hide them in the real hair. Leave it too late and you looked like a vain buzzard. He cinched his belt until it hurt and felt the small roll of fat with loathing. He made toast in the machine she had bought: five hundred and forty dollars. The bloody thing had twelve settings. Numbers one to six barely warmed the bread, seven and upwards charred it just as effectively as some twenty-five dollar piece of shit from Target.

He spread the blackened slices with cholesterol-lowering margarine and blood pressure-raising anchovy paste. Then he couldn't eat.

He went to his desk and switched on the computer. He didn't have to be at the university until eleven-thirty. What to do until then?

He had always written best at this time of day. It had come without effort.

What was the point of writing? He was a reject.

Rejected by the publishing world after fourteen novels. He had never been rejected. Published at twenty-three, never rejected.

Was Carter mad? What about the others? Of course, they'd taken their cue from Hillary & Woolfe. When Marjorie came around, they knew H & W had dumped him. If he wasn't good enough for H & W, why should they touch him?

What had Marjorie told them? He should have asked her. She wasn't dumb enough to tell them Carter didn't want the book. Why hadn't she told him before she went hawking the thing around? He could have told her what to say: 'Vincent's unhappy with H & W. He now thinks it was a mistake to listen to Adam Carter's promises. He's been shockingly published for one of Australia's modern masters.'

For a modern master. If the *New York Review of Books* called you a modern master, you were one, even if the reviewer also mentioned two vastly overrated pricks. And one of them was a one-book wonder and only that because his nauseating title, *The Lost Philosophy of Sock Knitting,* had for some reason appealed to thousands of cretins.

A reject. Writer of a book that wasn't good enough to be published unless he accepted an advance of five thousand pounds from some obscure porn publisher. An insult. Haig's bloody studio had cost ten times that.

Beloved of the French critics, winner of the Prix de Goncourt. Deserved favourite for the Booker passed over in favour of a vapid English navel picker. Three times cheated of the Miles Franklin by parochial, provincial idiots. How could it end like this?

The postman on his infuriating machine. Duncan went out. Four letters. The telephone bill. The power bill. A letter from the bank. They wanted the mortgage reduced by two hundred thousand dollars or he would be handed over to Collections.

Oh Lord. You couldn't write in circumstances like these. Between them, Gus and Merill-Streep had destroyed a major talent.

This could be from Brown. He loved the attention he got there, the intelligent, attractive young people. Sharp, in awe. Not Brown. The Mountain Workshop hadn't asked him back yet either.

Did the Americans know? Shouldn't the invitations have arrived by now? Age was a terrible thing, everything telescoping, accelerating. March. The annual US trip was only four months away. Haig said she didn't want to come this year.

Vincent, I hate being an appendage.

Well, she'd been pleased to be a bloody appendage in the early days. She'd hung onto him, touched him, kissed his cheek, his ear, put a hand in his pocket, she'd made sure the students knew who was the lover of the modern master, who was the chosen woman.

Duncan focused, found himsef looking at the two-metre-high painting on the wall opposite, the painting from Haig's joint exhibition after she finished art school. He'd had his eye on her since they were introduced at some lit festival thing. She'd been dressed like a French roadmender, a very appealing look. On opening night, he bought all five of her works. The next night, he took her to dinner and later to the suite in the Connell.

All that had remained was to ease Gus off the scene. They barely spoke, anyway. He couldn't waste any more of his life on her.

He made her a very generous offer. In an email from New York. That seemed to be a sensible way to do it. It avoided the unprofitable emotions that could be generated in a personal encounter.

How could he have known that the dreamy, palely loitering poet would in an instant turn into a slit-eyed money-grubbing vixen? Her solicitor, frightening feminist Alvina Raicheva, kicked off with an ambit claim to half of everything he had. Fortunately, the man-hating lawbitch's search for concealed assets failed to turn up his foreign earnings in the Banque Pétain.

But Gus ended up with half of what they could find. He had to borrow six hundred thousand dollars to buy her alleged share of the house.

Two hundred thousand dollars or Collections?

Duncan stared at Haig's painting. It was crap, a piece of imitation Kiefer, which made it second-generation crap. Some of the brownish blobs stuck to the canvas had hairs in them and bone fragments and what looked like pale bits of sinew too tough for stomach acid.

Haig thought she owed her career to talent. She didn't know that he'd arranged for two dealers to bid against each other when he'd put two of her paintings into an auction at Looby's. It cost a fortune but the sharp operators of the art world sat up. Suddenly she was collectable. Her career took off. And he got his money back with interest when the ghastly things were bought by art dupes for large sums at auction again a year later.

They hadn't screwed in some months now, more like three. And the last time was pretty perfunctory stuff, she'd been in the shower inside four minutes. You got more time from a hotel hooker.

Now that he thought about it, sex and her use of the studio upstairs had tapered off at around the same time. She'd fallen out of love with the studio he'd had built, the bloody thing cantilevered out into space, the light controlled by electronic blinds. She now did her creating in a former asylum, a building full of talentless canvas defacers, mostly young, a few ancient poseurs wearing neckerchiefs.

He would have to ring Marjorie. She was his only hope. A quick apology would do it. Shock, heat of the moment, grovel to her. He pressed the numbers. She answered at the second ring.

'Marjorie, my dear . . .'

'Bugger off, Vincent. Don't call me, I'll call you.'

His computer pinged. Email.

From Marjorie.

It is with regret that I must inform you that I have decided to terminate our agency agreement as of . . .

He'd have to sell the house. Rent? Vincent Duncan renting a house? His precious furniture, his books in a rented house? That was not thinkable.

The phone rang.

Marjorie, the cow, she'd be full of regret now, he would be in charge. He let it ring, stroked his stubble.

'Yes,' he said.

'Glenys from uni, Vincent. Just a reminder you've got Sarius Godber's one-on-one at eleven. And Dr Truss wants a minute after you've finished.'

'I'll see him if I've got time before lunch,' said Duncan.

'He wants to see you today.'

'Wants? Wants? Do I detect a command?'

Glenys sighed. 'He asked me to tell you to see him after your student meeting.'

'Truss told you to *tell* me?'

'Ah, yes, Vincent.'

'Well, *tell* the acting head of department to make a bloody appointment to see me.'

He put the phone down.

The brainless, illiterate little poseur.

No newly arrived twat from Adelaide who'd published a book called *Contestation and Transcendence: The Body in Seijin Manga* was going to summon Vincent Duncan like a junior lecturer. The whole department should fall to its knees every morning to give thanks that Vincent Duncan was on the staff. He gave respectability to the degrees they awarded to sensitive, pop-eyed, dirty-haired, late-developers for writing sub-David Foster Wallace tripe.

You couldn't fail the unread scribblers because that meant reading their rubbish and commenting on it. And if you did fail them, they went sobbing to the likes of Truss and he had their efforts re-examined by some lick-spittle guaranteed to pass them.

Duncan made the journey to the university. The feeling of power the small, thrusting Mini John Cooper Works gave him always cheered him up. He parked in the deputy vice chancellor's space. Why not? She wasn't using it.

In his office, he read the first four pages of Sarius Godber's second draft of her novel. It was like eating deep-fried cheesecake, but, to his amazement, there were three or four acceptable passages. Even a hint of irony. Sarius arrived, dressed like a rock climber. He gave her his twenty-minute lecture on irony, told her the work was promising but the mid-section needed reimagining. Novels turned on their mid-sections. Etc.

She nodded throughout, taking notes, and went off glowing. She really wasn't bad looking. A hard body.

A day's work done.

He found Dr Leon Truss toying with his earring. He was wearing a black T-shirt with the words LOVE YOURSELF A LITTLE on his chest.

'Vincent, mate!' said Truss. 'Thanks for dropping in.'

'I'm not dropping in,' said Duncan. 'I was ordered to present myself to your Royal Acting HOD Highness.'

'Oh nonsense,' said Truss. 'Complete misunderstanding. I simply wanted to have a little chat. About things.'

'What things?'

'A couple of things, actually. Trivial stuff.'

'Don't trifle with me. I've seen your PhD. *Humiliation, Pain, Pleasure and the Quest for Personal Identity.*'

'Vincent, that is pure, pure aggression. Can you bring yourself to not see every one-on-one we have as a cage-fighting bout?'

'It would be a bad mismatch,' said Duncan.

'Yes, well, firstly, we were thinking, just thinking idly, you understand . . .'

'The idleness of your thinking,' said Duncan, 'I understand perfectly.'

Truss's right hand stroked the left in a loving, comforting way.

'Vincent, we were thinking that since you only use your large office a few hours of the day, an average of one point six actually and that's during term . . .'

'Have you been spying on me, Truss?'

'Please, don't be paranoid,' said Truss. 'It's Rump.'

'Rump?'

'The Resources Utilisation Monitoring Program? It's been discussed at staff meetings, Vincent. Where colleagues meet. The cornerstone of the collegial tradition. We'd so love you to pop in on one when your outside commitments allow.'

'Rump my arse. Spying on the staff.'

'So. We were thinking that, going forward, your office would comfortably house four staff units. That's you and Meredith, Jude and Roberta.'

'Who the hell is Roberta?'

'Ah. When he gets back from long-service, Bob is Roberta. Didn't he tell you?'

'We've never talked about quests for personal identity,' said Duncan, 'that end with the subtraction of two testicles and the addition of a single vowel.'

Truss smiled, showing an alarming amount of gum. 'Cruel wit undulled,' he said. 'That's so good to see in older people. So it's settled, then. On the same page re resource utilisation.'

'My answer, Trussboy,' said Duncan, the words hissing through his teeth, 'is that I will not share *my* office, that's *MY* office, with Meredith, Jude or anyone else, surgically and chemically regendered or not. Is that clear to you? Are we on the same bloody Adelaide Protestant guilt-ridden hymnsheet?'

Truss put his palms together and bowed his head in a humble eastern non-Protestant way.

'Vincent,' he said, 'I'm really, really sad that you can't embrace the department's inclusive and egalitarian ethic. So it's my sad, sad duty to say that we will have to discuss whether to renew your contract.'

Duncan controlled his need to lean across the desk and take the man by his long lizardy throat and squeeze the life out of him, see his tongue come out, his face turn purple, the capillaries in his skin pop.

'I think you'll find,' said Duncan, 'that my contract has years to run.'

'I think you'll find that the years have slipped by,' said Truss. 'It has one term left to run. I can say that the feeling in the department is its expiry presents an opportunity for change and renewal. For both parties, of course.'

Duncan tried to slam the door on his way out. But Truss had placed a little rubber wedge against the door jamb.

In the Mini, Duncan considered his situation. A brilliant career in the balance. No: ended. Usurers demanding two hundred thousand dollars or his house. The prospect of sucking up to the entire department, man, woman and those on the plane to Thailand, or losing the large sum that appeared in his bank account every fortnight.

Haig. She could provide the breathing space. Two sell-out exhibitions, forty-odd assemblages of animal, vegetable and mineral substances shifted to the gullible at ludicrous prices. Even subtracting the criminal commission taken by her gallery, she'd have a stash of several hundred grand. She certainly contributed nothing to the household.

A loan. He would propose the transaction as a loan, a short-term loan while accountants were dragging their heels transferring massive sums to him.

He rang her mobile: the answering service. He would have to go to her chamber of horrors in the former asylum.

The Alfa was in the parking area. He couldn't find a space, so he occupied the loading zone. He'd been here once for some art-world function.

Except for two Coles shopping trolleys, the entrance hall was empty. Up the stairs and last door on the left was his recollection.

The place smelled of dope, turpentine, burnt pasta sauce, welding gases and, faintly, of ancient urine containing old-fashioned pacifying drugs. From somewhere came weird electronic music with an unsettling pulse beat.

A card on the door: H. Alexander.

He tried the handle. Locked. He knocked. Knocked again. Again and louder.

It opened a crack. Haig, sleepy, wearing a T-shirt and track pants.

'Having a nap,' she said. 'What do you want?'

He should show interest. 'Thought I'd see what you were working on,' said Duncan.

'Vincent, you know I don't like . . .'

'Oh, come on,' he said, 'don't be shy.'

He pushed the door open and went in, began a tour of the works in progress. One featured thick-painted male figures wearing plastic shopping bags, bubble wrap and strips of hessian. Another appeared to be composed of blowtorched plastic toys – dolls, cars, guns – and what were possibly sex aids of a phallic nature.

'Interesting,' said Duncan. 'I sense change and renewal.'

He was passing a door and he opened it.

A pale-skinned young man was lying on a blow-up camping mattress. He was naked, tumescent, smoking a cigarette and reading a comic book.

'Hi,' he said.

'Vincent, this is David,' said Haig from behind Duncan. 'He, ah, he's modelling for me. David, this is Vincent Duncan.'

David gave a little wave with his cigarette.

'My mum loves your books,' he said, in a respectful way.

Given a gun, Duncan would have left him bleeding on the deflating mattress, dying in his own blood, cadmium red, deep hue.

'Enjoy your comic,' said Duncan and closed the door.

He continued the tour. Icy calm was required. This could work to his advantage in several ways. At the door, he said, 'See me out.'

They went down the stairs in silence, into the day.

'I see a very powerful show coming up,' said Duncan. 'Very, very strong. An added depth and maturity. Painful with insight.'

Haig was combing her hair with her fingers. 'Thank you,' she said.

'My pleasure. Listen, I need a little loan from you,' he said, no hint of neediness in his voice. 'The bank's being awkward and the accountant's two months behind with a very large cheque.'

'How much?' said Haig.

'Just two hundred grand. Short-term loan. Bridging finance. A few weeks.'

'Two hundred thousand dollars?'

'That'll do. Two hundred, two-fifty.'

She stared at him. When had her lips become so thin?

'Vincent, I can't lend you *twenty* thousand,' she said. 'I've bought a place in Liguria. Somewhere to escape to. Liguria is very expensive.'

She turned and went up the stairs. Barefoot. He hadn't noticed that. At the top, she turned and flashed teeth at him. 'Ask the bank for time, darling.'

Duncan drove home. It was lunchtime, no breakfast, he should eat.

He opened a bottle of Mumm's and took it and a glass onto the terrace. Waiting for the end.

Shall I pluck a flower, boys, shall I save or spend?

All turns sour, boys, waiting for the end.

He sipped and watched the light on the water. Betrayed by everyone. All the wasted years, the words torn from his soul. Tears formed in his eyes, swelled, broke, ran down his cheeks.

The phone. He went in, sniffing.

'Vincent, dear man.'

Marjorie.

'Vincent, marvellous, marvellous news,' she said. 'You've won the Claris Buckhard Prize for Uplifting Fiction.'

'The what?'

'The Claris Buckhard Prize for Uplifting Fiction.'

'For what?'

'For your fabulous new book. For *A Reducing Fire*.'

Uplifting fiction?

A Reducing Fire uplifting fiction? Were they barking mad? It was a cry of existential despair, it was the plaintive hopeless howl of the last polar bear on the last, melting ice floe.

'I know, I know, a prize under the radar, darling,' said Marjorie. 'Our clever Emily had the bright idea to send them all our unpublished manuscripts. It's new, this is the first year. It's Canadian.'

Oh Lord. The Canadian Country Women's Association Prize for Uplifting Fiction. A framed certificate, a LumboJack chainsaw and a case of Brownie Bear's Best maple syrup.

'It's one million Canadian dollars, Vincent,' she said. 'And one million dollars to the creative writing institution of your choice.'

It took time to register.

Oh Lord, in your wisdom and mercy, you have given us this woman Clovis Hardbuck, whatever.

'But hold your breath,' said Marjorie. 'We're on a roll, darling. Cal Braverman at Random and Cissy Cowling at Harper both heard about it and they're in a dogfight.'

'A dogfight.' He was trying to be calm.

'Yes. A dogfight. Cal offered one million, Cissy said one-five and now Cal's coming back to me.'

Ah, the exquisite timing of it. The fearful symmetry.

'Marjorie,' he said, 'dear Marjorie, let me read something to you. *It is with regret that I must inform you that I have decided to terminate our agency agreement as of . . .* Heard enough, Marj, old girl? Old sausage?'

'Oh Vincent, don't be silly, just an impulsive foolishness. We've had so many little tiffs, haven't we? But we're still together. I've sent you an email on the subject, darling.'

'Fourth-rate piece of sentimental rubbish,' said Duncan. 'As I recall, *darling*, those were your words. Well, *darling*, since you've terminated yourself, you won't be getting fifteen exhorbitant per cent of my earnings derived from the fourth-rate piece of sentimental rubbish, will you?'

He listened to her pleading for a while, then he said, 'Kindly redirect Claret Hardacre and Random and HarperCollins to me. Goodbye, Marjorie. And my best to your boob of a husband.'

Back to the terrace with his mobile. Another glass of Mumm's. How sweet the song of the magpie. He dialled Truss's number.

'Hello, Painboy,' he said. 'Vincent Duncan. I thought you'd like to know that my new novel has won the Mavis Hardsuck Prize.'

'Very nice, Vincent,' said Truss. 'Some rural thing, is it? I'm in a meeeting, so if . . .'

'It comes with a million dollars for the creative writing institution of my choice. That's a million dollars, Truss-man.'

'A million dollars?'

'For the institution of my choice.'

'Lunch, Vincent, let's do lunch. I've just been telling the people in this room that I will fight to my last breath for the renewal of your contract.'

'Bye, bye, Trussiewuss.'

A refill. The golden liquid, the minute bubbles of gas entering the bloodstream. He rang Haig's mobile. She answered.

'Vincent Duncan,' he said. 'I want to say to you, you talentless bitch, that people only buy your hideous rubbish because I rigged an auction.'

Haig gasped.

'I also want to say, art harlot,' he said, 'that I am throwing all your possessions onto the pavement. Get your dickboy to park the Alfa outside my house or I'll get a court order.'

Duncan went to his study and found his list of students with phone numbers. Sarius Godber. A rock climber's body. Perhaps an invitation to supper at the Enoteca. They could talk about writing. His, hers. His, in the main.

His computer pinged. Email.

Cal Braverman? Cissy Cowling? Which dog in the fight? What advance on one point five million?

Marjorie, the poor cow.

Vincent: I'm afraid there's been a mistake. Manuscript cover pages swapped. The Buckhard winner is Amerine Panikbar for *A Quest of Flamingoes*. Sorry about that.

Marjorie

Through the window, he saw another magpie alight on the hand-cut Castlemaine bluestone paving.

6

Blackberries

Tom Keneally

Austin North stood before his best year ten class. The smart alecks in it were intellectual, verbal smart alecks. In contrast to the rootless imitations of American gangbangers he had to teach in other classrooms, here hardly anyone called each other *dude*.

Today all of them had their poetry books out and open on their desk.

– So, said Austin, this poet was a war correspondent during World War II, sending back news stories to the Australian papers from the Middle East . . .

He wrote '1939–1945' on the blackboard.

– You probably know those dates from history. Dates of profound meaning for the entire world. Early in the war a great number of ships were sunk, and the bodies of drowned sailors were washed ashore. The poet, Slessor, saw them on a beach in the Middle East, and of course they made an impact on him. Some of the dead were only a year or two older than you.

Despite themselves, they took in this idea.

– Notice there's a quietness, the hush of mourning, in those opening lines:

Softly and humbly to the Gulf of Arabs

The convoys of dead sailors come . . .

Peter Claxton (Mr Handsome) put his hand up. He was a champion sprinter and was that dangerous, snide combination, jock and brain. His athleticism doubled his confidence and accentuated his contempt for most teachers – not as authority figures but as intellects. I suppose I'm lucky, Austin thought. He only half-despises me.

– How is it, sir, asked Claxton with mock submission, that he says 'humbly'? How can they be humble when they're dead?

– It's a metaphor, of course. The bodies wash up and down in the tide as if they're not sure they belong on the beach. Whereas *softly* is a more direct adverb . . .

– Because they probably are soft, poor things, said Angela Yankovich, a bright kid who was a member of some evangelical church group, at least for now. Austin had a feeling that it wouldn't last. In six months time she would forget all that and be the girlfriend of some town hoon whom she'd think the smartest thing she'd ever met and who might steal her future from her.

– Exactly right, said Austin, more to reinforce her than because she had got the point of the poem.

– Why can't you sum it up for us in about fifty words, sir? asked Peter Claxton, just for the sake of mischief. That's all we need. We can take it down and be fine in the exam.

– Poetry isn't just for exams, Austin told them as they knew he'd tell them, and some of the boys groaned at that, as he knew they would. You'll all be poets sooner or later. Because let me tell you, poets are no different from you and me. The day will come when you'll try to be like them yourself. And if you succeed, you won't be on a pedestal somewhere. You'll still need to buy your groceries and scrub your floor. Shaw Neilson was a messenger in the public service and earned less than the clerks. If you'd seen him on the street in Sydney you wouldn't have taken notice of him – he'd be scurrying along, wearing a suit but not a very good one. Then David Campbell – David Campbell was a World War II fighter pilot and then went back to sheep farming. When it came to farming you couldn't tell the difference between him and any other farmer. But he happened to write some of the best poems ever written on earth about cattle and sheep and pastures and living on a farm. And then Judith Wright – I heard her speak once. She had a scratchy old voice like somebody's aunt. She was just a school teacher. It was when she began speaking that you forgot all that and became enchanted.

One of the boys at the back, who had a reputation as a rugby league player in a town which had produced many famed players and test cricketers (for some reason batsmen rather than bowlers), put his hand up and asked, If poets are ordinary, sir, wouldn't you make a good poet?

There was some affection in that, and a roar of laughter in the room.

– Ha-ha, said Austin North when the noise subsided. But I don't have the talent, you see. I don't have that hidden quality that's needed. I don't have the fire that could allow me to write, *Softly and humbly to the Gulf of Arabs*... If I'd been born then and saw the same things Slessor saw, I would write something like, *Dear Mum, it's sad to see how many dead sailors are washing up because of U-boat activity.* You see the difference now?

They did. He could see they did. Austin had a reputation as an excellent English teacher. Even the kids who pretended to get nothing out of his classes often got plenty. It was a game they played, him and them, arguing the usefulness of poetry year by year. He enjoyed the tussle – it was better than having a class full of obedient automatons who took notes frantically. And in every class, you saw a girl here, a boy there, suddenly becoming intoxicated with words. *Softly and humbly*...

• •

Softly and humbly – about five years past – there appeared on the main street on Fridays or Saturday mornings angular people of anthracite black, the women swathed in a white which swept over their heads as well as covering their bodies to the ankles. Their children with them – obediently so – they loped along with that African, rhythmic walk, while townspeople – dependent on their attitude – watched them go with fascination or with fear of their strangeness. These people were the Sudanese refugees who had settled here in numbers you didn't see elsewhere in the bush.

Actually, as Austin would discover, they were the Southern Sudanese. They were people whose plight was so undeniable that Australia had let them settle here.

One of them spoke at the Anglican Men's night. He was a highly educated Southern Sudanese who had fled with his parents from a refugee camp and crossed the border into Ethiopia. From there the family had travelled to Egypt, where the speaker, who used a precise, pleasantly accented English, studied engineering. He had come to Australia not as a refugee – the way most of his fellow Sudanese had come – but under a scheme that brought in technocrats who had areas of expertise in which Australia was short-handed.

– But though I have had a different history, he said, I take a great interest in my brethren. My wife and I belong to the local Sudanese committee, which helps the refugees settle in and gives them some background into Australian culture.

– Whenever I speak to civic groups, the Sudanese engineer went on, I plead with them for every tolerance. Because my fellow countrymen have been through terrible times. Their mothers and sisters have been subjected to every indignity including, in some cases, violation – all by the Arab militias the government in Khartoum arms. In many cases fathers have been shot before their children's eyes. The sons, as young as seven or eight, have been forced to take up arms either by the Sudanese Liberation Army, the Sudanese People's Liberation Front, or other groups. Some have been taken away by the Arab militias and sold as slaves to farmers in the borderlands between north and south. On top of that, they have seen their grain barns burned down and their cattle taken away, so they have starved as well – the younger children giving way to fevers and often perishing.

– On top of that, they have also been in refugee camps, and there, while they lived in UNICEF tents or under blue plastic, the people who exploited them in the outside world simply went on exploiting them there. So now, even in Australia, it is hard for them to expect there is not some terrible danger just around the corner.

Austin had heard that speech a few years ago. He occasionally met the Sudanese engineer in the street – his name, which Austin hadn't caught when the man spoke at the church, was David Malwai. *David*, because most of the Sudanese were Coptic Christians. Even David, Austin thought, was as watchful as he had said in his lecture his less lucky Southern Sudanese brothers and sisters were.

To Austin, the interesting thing about the Sudanese was that they confused the normal racial uncertainties of the town. Though some of the boys were starting to play at forming gangs, so far they were better behaved than some of the Aboriginal young, whose acts of vandalism and robbery kept the town edgy. But where did they fit, these faces dark as night with their glittering huge eyes?

• •

On the morning of a day that had begun with a fierce winter frost Austin was teaching his year tens when the headmaster knocked on his door, which had a plain glass panel in it. Through this glass Austin could see the headmaster and, behind him, one of the willowy Sudanese, a young woman, huge-eyed, bare-headed and wearing the school uniform. Austin stepped off his rostrum to go to let them in. As a hubbub from the desks arose, he turned to repress it.

– Come on, this isn't an RSL club, he said.

Interestingly, he had a capacity for absolute command. He was lucky that way, because he thought that in this tough new age he couldn't have been a teacher without it. The noise reduced itself to an acceptable whisper. He opened the classroom door.

The headmaster said, Mr North, this is Miriam Salong.

The girl wore an exceptionally long school tunic which fell far below her knees.

The headmaster handed Austin the appropriate paperwork.

– Because Miriam's a refugee and English isn't her first language, she's a little older than the members of your class. I am sure you will have a great deal of success teaching her.

– Thank you, said Austin.

The headmaster wasn't such a bad fellow and occasionally took Austin to the bowling club for a drink. But at the door of his classroom they kept up this formal claptrap.

– Very well, Mr North, said the headmaster.

– Come through, Miss Salong, Austin told the girl.

The girl, head down, passed by him and entered the classroom. She stood looking lost by the rostrum. The headmaster confided in Austin.

– She doesn't have textbooks yet. You know the Sudanese engineer? David someone? David will have them for her by tomorrow.

– Okay.

– Well, I'll leave you and Miriam to it.

And he turned away.

Austin closed the door and leaned against its frame. There was an empty desk next to one of the reliable kids, a girl named Denise, a farmer's daughter.

– Miriam, you can take that seat there. Can she share your textbook, Denise?

The pleasant child called Denise nodded. Miriam Salong glided through the class with a walk they could not teach at anybody's modelling school. Austin was waiting for one of the class yobbos to whistle at her. It did not happen, at least, not yet. Her presence, her unchanging expression, got her in her long tunic all the way down the classroom and into her chair.

On that day and others he was conscious, at least part of the time, of teaching to what he imagined Miriam Salong's standard of English to be. Sentences he would normally not reprise he would now go over in the simplest English he could find. Perhaps that's what he should always have done. Perhaps it was good to have a disadvantaged child – and if David could be believed, this girl was disadvantaged – in the class, to get you out of lazy formulations. This girl brought him to hone his pedagogic skills.

• •

Austin North's marriage to Meredith North, *nee* Crawford, was a ruggedly happy one. Meredith was a very practical woman – even their courtship had been practical; she knew the pay scales for various grades of teachers and for subject masters, and thus what Austin and she could expect in life. These terms of employment were very nearly her endearments. She was the most honest woman alive: president of the local netball association, vice-president of Little Athletics, and the mother who always had the sliced-up oranges and the bandaids for junior rugby. She worked as the reserves and parks manager in the local shire council, that is, she commanded all playing fields and recreation spaces in the region. The North's two pleasant children went to the other high school in town – they preferred to explain why they didn't go to Austin's school rather than why they did.

Austin had never thought that a marriage should be more than his, and he certainly knew a great number that were less. He and Meredith could still be hungry for each other and Meredith's sensuality, once aroused, astonished and gratified him.

But now, for no reason he could explain or feel guilty for, Miriam's presence in the classroom gave him acute delight. No other student had ever had this influence on him. If one of the seven classes a week in which he taught her happened to be the last before lunchtime or the last of the day, he would keep her a few minutes, looking at her written work. He knew it was contrary to the modern, unlegislated school code to detain her longer than that. Now that girls matured so early and adopted the manners of grown women, people had developed antennae for infatuations between teachers and students.

He was delighted her English proved somewhat better than he'd suspected.

– Miriam, he asked her before letting her leave one day, what do you plan to do when you leave school?

– I want to be a nurse, she said with her inimitable accent, her gleaming, vast eyes looking away.

– So you'll stay on and do your Higher School Certificate?

– Yes, Mr David told my parents I should stay.

– So your mother and father are with you here in Australia? he asked.

– Yes, she said. But her eyes blazed slowly with doubt about what his question might mean.

– And do you have brothers and sisters?

– Two brothers. They go at St Paul's.

It was the Catholic Primary School.

– Ah, pardon me asking, he said. It's just that . . . well, I'm a friend of David Malwai too.

– Yes, she said. He is giving me my books.

He nodded, told her she could go and watched her walk like a gazelle to the door. As easily as she strode, she still had that expectation of ambush.

He had given the class a poem called 'Drifters' by Bruce Dawe, Dawe being a man who understood ordinary people and wrote in transparent language. It took very little, so Austin thought, to open up one of his poems to the kids.

The first line was so clear: *One day soon he'll tell her it's time to start packing...*

The resultant essays from the class turned out, in the case of his two best students, Angela Yankovich and Peter Claxton, to be first-rate, though in an exam-passing, fairly stand-offish way. The poem was a formula to them, to be solved like an equation in maths or physics. Amongst the rest, Miriam's was the only remarkable piece of writing – it wasn't at all in this case because of his willingness to accept as dazzling all the utterances of his object of fascination. By objective standards it showed oddity and wisdom and courage.

Her essay read:

Bruce Dawe is an Australian poet and he knows people are forced to move from place to place and it is sometimes an exciting thing to the innocent children but is full of sorrow for the parents. This is a small poem of only thirteen lines, but he tells us in it the whole story of moving from one place to another and also not to be able to stay. Not to say I might or I mightn't go. But to say I must. So at first in this poem when the father says it is time to start packing the children are excited crying, 'Truly?' and they make the dog excited who dashes around. But the mother must make ready for the journey. She goes to where the vegetables grow and picks up all the green tomatoes from the vines. Then she sees her oldest daughter. She is the one who knows the mother does not want to go. And the oldest daughter is the one who wants to stay too for she was happy here. But the youngest daughter wasn't.

The mother has a bottling set – which is bottles fruit is put in and stored. She never unpacked it from the last house they had in a town named Grovedale. She takes the set with her. When the truck is loaded up they go past the blackberries and she remembers that when they came to this house she picked all the blackberries off the blackberry bushes. Then she put out her hands and said to her husband to make a wish. The wish she hoped him to make was that they would stay here. This is because it is hard to go from place to place to place . . .

As for punctuation, thought Austin, it could be looked at in happier days.

· ·

William Butler Yeats had a poem, a short one, in which he asked as an old man how – with a particularly handsome girl sitting across from him – he could discourse learnedly on European politics? Austin North understood that poem now with a new intensity. How could he teach, with that girl sitting there? He managed, though. Except for the sentences he styled particularly for her, he performed his old tricks, on automatic pilot, automatic pedagogy.

One day Austin North was – by accident – walking behind her in the corridor when a group of boys from year eleven rushed from behind him and overtook Miriam in her long tunic. Something about them made him quicken his step. And after the boys got beyond her they turned round to face her, all grinning, not seeing Austin because their focus and their lust lay so hard on her.

One asked her, Have you had an Australian root yet, Miriam?

Austin heard. He was overtaken by an irrational fury unfamiliar to him, someone else's rage. Something that had never happened within these walls. In his courtship of Meredith he had never reached such a state of possessiveness as this. And it was instantaneous, as he'd reflect afterwards, achieved in nano-seconds.

Half-uncomprehending, Miriam edged past the boys as Austin caught up with them. He took hold of the tie and some of the shirt front of the boy who'd mocked Miriam. His name was Grice. The son of Pete Grice, who owned a BP franchise and roadhouse at the southern approaches to town. On parent–teacher nights Grice and his wife moved woodenly from table to table, Austin remembered. Now, for the first time in his history, he had rammed a boy up against the wall. Fortuitously, Grice's shoulder missed one of the old iron coat hooks – older than any of the staff – still attached there.

What did you say? Austin asked the boy.

He could see the kid was bewildered. Is this Mr North? the boy was asking himself. This was the sort of thing that could be expected of the more overtly disciplinarian teachers but not from Mr North. Maybe for this reason, the boy couldn't speak. Freckles were blazing out in the pallor of his face.

– I heard what you said, Austin shouted. If I catch you again, or any of your mates, I'll have you suspended. I'll watch you all the time, and one word . . . one word . . .

By now embarrassment began to settle on him. Like anyone in that situation, he tried to justify himself, to gild the lily, by repetition.

– You can't speak to a girl that way. Do you understand?

The incident had so frightened him that he believed for a while it had cured his infatuation. But he woke at three o'clock the following morning in a frenzy, both of shame and obsession. This is Nabokov, he thought. How could that have happened? He was as crazy as Humbert Humbert. He'd read *Lolita* and felt smart and superior, above Humbert's folly. Could one imagine falling for a child when there were so many robust women, including Meredith? The idea disgusted him and only Nabokov's reputation and the fame of the book muted his distaste in a small way.

He got to school very early that morning, unlocked and locked the main door and walked the child-free corridors to the staffroom. He had always liked entering the school building when it was not operating for its ordained purpose, when its stillness gave it an atmosphere of abandonment.

He set to work marking year eleven History, but it was hard to focus. He was afraid that the Grice boy might complain to his parents, and his parents complain to the headmaster. If that *didn't* happen, he felt he might be able to forget his shame one day. Irrational, of course, and shameful as well. Because what he was guilty of in Grice's case he was guilty of, and a lack of punishment wasn't the point. But he had entered a world where getting away with things was what counted.

• •

Almost according to racial stereotype, Miriam had become a gift to the high school track and field team. Austin found out about this quite accidentally, through a passage in the school news sheet pinned to the staffroom bulletin board.

The passage read: *The track and field team has found a new star in Miriam Salong, who has been at the school only one term. She is a natural runner who at last Saturday's athletics meeting against the girls of St Brigid's Catholic High School won the 1500 metres and broke the school record by 4.7 seconds. Congratulations, Miriam.*

There was no remission of sins for Austin. About a quarter past eight an early-arriving girl was at the door with a note.

– Austin, it said, could you drop in before class starts?

It was unsigned but it was in the headmaster's writing.

He thanked the girl, went across the room, closed up the essay he was working on, put it back in the folder and put all the essays in his briefcase. He set off and felt nauseated by this foreshadowing of chastisement.

He walked into the office where Mrs Wallace, the school secretary, was just taking off her jacket.

– The boss says he wants to see me, Austin explained.

And then he remembered to observe the automatic etiquette.

– How are you going, Mrs Wallace, anyhow?

– My husband's off work with the back, she said. Whine, whine, whine. Boss's in there.

She nodded towards the office, its door closed. Nonetheless, the headmaster called, Come in.

Austin entered. What mysterious compound ensured that headmasters' offices smelled just the same as when he was a child – a compound of dust, envelopes, varnish and knowingness?

– Austin, said the headmaster, as rosy cheeked, authoritative and ready for the day as a headmaster in a film. Sit down.

Austin did, his back arched. The headmaster picked up a student file and frowned into it before putting it down.

– There's a problem with a student.

Austin's face burned ridiculously.

– It's that Sudanese girl in your year ten. The new PE teacher – Craig, you know, who coaches the team –

invited her to run against St Brigid's and she turned up in her school uniform. One of the girls offered her the use of an athletic kit – those little shorts they wear these days? But she wouldn't put it on. She ran in her school uniform, won the race and broke the school record. With all that navy blue serge flapping around her knees. The girls at St Brigid's were laughing at her, but she soon put them in their place. But there's another meeting against the grammar school this weekend. Craig says she'll be a state champion in the proper gear.

All Austin's uneasy blood returned to its normal channels and he was fascinated and challenged by what he was hearing. He uttered one or two vowels of laughter and then shook his head. He was adapting himself to the idea of his object of infatuation as an athlete.

– So I remembered, said the headmaster, that you know that Sudanese engineer. David, is it? I wondered if you could ask David to ask the parents – sorry, a bit circuitous – ask them do they have any objections to her wearing normal gear? A state champion wouldn't be unwelcome. When you talk to this David . . . what's his name?

– David Malwai, said Austin.

– Well, when you talk to him, show him this picture.

He handed a photograph of a freckled girl of about fourteen to Austin. The kid in the picture wore a blousey T-shirt rather than the tight vest other girls in the track and field team wore, and bloomery shorts rather than the legless shorts, near-bikini bottoms, that were now favoured.

– This is Megan Wishart. You know, her parents are members of the Evangelical Brethren. Ask your engineer to see if Miriam's parents would think this sort of thing is okay.

Since it involved him in the question of Miriam, Austin took the Megan Wishart photograph gratefully. He put the picture away in the breast pocket of his sports coat. He felt ecstatic.

Back in the staffroom he looked up and called David Malwai's work number. He was put through to David's extension but a voice asked him to leave a message. Austin said he didn't like troubling him at work. He explained the situation. Could they perhaps have a coffee at the Arcade Coffee Shop at, say, five-thirty?

A message was waiting for him at lunchtime. David couldn't meet him today, but could tomorrow.

Austin rang him back and said that was soon enough.

• •

Meredith was a demon for dry-cleaning and energetically looked after the rejuvenation of all the North family's clothing. When the slightest drop of inappropriate fluid – gravy or, in Austin's case, wine – fell upon the fabric, she would steal his children's sport kits, school uniforms, and Austin's suit and jackets and slacks for what Austin considered a premature cleaning.

The next morning the children had already gone off to school, and Meredith had in her hands Austin's sports coat to add to a pile of clothes – hers, the kids – she would drop into the dry cleaners on the way to work. She had had to empty the pockets, and had found the photograph of Megan Wishart in her 1950s running kit.

– Who's this kid? she asked.

It was obviously something that required reasonable explanation. A rational plan even if a multi-linked one – the headmaster asked him to ask David Malwai to ask Miriam's parents if they would let their daughter run in such gear, whether it was, according to their custom, modest enough.

But he found he had a fierce reluctance to utter Miriam's name in front of Meredith. It would be a form of exposure. And so, with the quick-footed deception practised by men obsessed with someone other than their wives, he told her another story.

– Oh, that's Megan Wishart. She's the school champion four hundred–metre runner.

– Plain little thing, said Meredith, looking at the child's pan of a face and her blizzard of freckles. Meredith cocked one eyebrow and looked at him from beneath it. You're not turning into one of those funny old men, are you?

– I've been a funny old man for a long time, he said, grinning.

– You know what I mean. Though this is an extremely plain child. Linda's so lucky with her looks.

– That's not the point, he said, as if he was standing up for feminism. She gave it to me yesterday. There's that school bulletin board outside the headmaster's office, and we pin up pictures of kids who've excelled some way in the past couple of weeks. This girl's parents are devout Evangelicals – that's why she's dressed like a 1950s sprinter. She doesn't want to put it there herself – in case they find out that she's being prideful. So she gave it to me yesterday and said, if it weren't too proudful of me, I could put it on the bulletin board. You see, she won the four hundred metres against St Brigid's.

– Why would she pick you?

– Because she knew full well I'd put it on the bulletin board. Because I'm an easy mark. That's why.

– You're certainly an easy mark, she confirmed. Little tart!

Having completed the pile of dry cleaning, she even stepped forward and kissed him.

– Oh, I've got to have coffee with David Malwai at five-thirty, he remembered to tell her. About the Sudanese kids at school.

– Don't worry, said Meredith, I won't be home much before you.

Their daughter, Linda, who was as competent as her mother, would probably have the dinner on by then.

The afternoon sky had turned steely above the town and he was pleased to be out of the wind when he walked into the Arcade Coffee Shop. David Malwai was already there, reading the *Sydney Morning Herald* with all the scholarliness of a judge reading a legal judgement. David noticed Austin from a metre away, and folded the paper, rose and shook hands. There was always this courtliness about him.

– And your wife and children? asked David Malwai in his faintly accented English.

Austin said they were well.

– I think it's wonderful the way your Sudanese committee looks after everyone, from the parents to the children.

– So how is Miriam?

– Magnificent! he wanted to say. Celestial! Beyond utterance! The most beautiful girl I have seen, an innate intelligence blazing in her eyes. A transcendent addition to the family of the Commonwealth of Australia!

He said instead, Her English is better than I thought.

– Yes, said David. They had an English teacher in the refugee camp outside Khartoum. Her parents say that other children flitted in and out of it and got disheartened, but this teacher took Miriam under his wing. With the results you see.

Austin felt immediately jealous of this idealistic teacher – no doubt young, to try a job like that. Was he English, American, Egyptian, Sudanese? Questions that couldn't be asked here, of course.

– You know, the camps are dangerous and demoralising places. The family would have a lot of time for the southern liberation movements. But there are extremists amongst them, and they police the camps according to their convenience, not that of ordinary refugees. People would find their sons in ditches with their throats cut. For dissenting.

Austin was shocked. Innocent Westerners thought of the camps as havens, secure places, not a continuation of the anguish.

As he was accustoming himself to this idea the woman came along to take his order, an interruption for which he was grateful. She was the mother of one of his kids so they were able to talk about that, a conversation with an overworked woman in a country town in New South Wales compensating for the suspect enthusiasm of a young, unknown teacher in Sudan.

– He's getting on very well, said Austin of the woman's son, the future lawyer, she was thinking, the doctor, the High Court judge. Sometimes it was so easy to make people happy, and sometimes it was the work of a lifetime. The woman went off beaming to get his long black coffee. She was so grateful that when it came back there was a free Anzac biscuit on the side of the coffee cup.

Now he explained to David Malwai that Miriam was a talented runner, but she insisted on running in her school tunic, which was longer than most other girls' to begin with. She'd still broken the school fifteen hundred–metre record by nearly five seconds.

He pulled out the picture of Megan Wishart.

– The headmaster wondered could you ask Miriam's father whether this sort of gear would be okay for his daughter to run in? As you see, it's very modest. The girl in the picture is a strict Christian.

The engineer studied the picture for a long time.

– I think the school would like a fairly early answer, said Austin.

David looked up.

– Well, I could take it and show them, but I think you should come, too. You can give the meeting a sort of authority.

– When? asked Austin.

– Sunday morning after church. They finish about eleven a.m.

– The Catholic church?

Because he knew from Google that the Southern Sudanese were likely to be Coptic Christians, which was not far from Catholicism.

– They prefer the Anglican church. You see, it's High Church. The minister wears all the vestments. He even has incense. So they go there. And then they stay on and have a Coptic prayer meeting.

Austin said, I think the phys ed teacher would like us to see them earlier than that. There's another athletics meeting on Saturday, with the grammar school.

– Well, maybe tomorrow evening or the next day, said David. I'll have to ask them and call you.

– You can leave a message at the school, said Austin. I'll tell them to expect one.

They finished their coffees, shook hands formally and parted. If David Malwai has Australian-born children, he thought, what will he make of their slap-dash manners picked up in the schoolyard?

He got a call at school from David Malwai the following afternoon. They could meet the Salong family the following night at eight o'clock.

– I should tell you that the Salongs might not be enthusiastic about sport. Indifferent, I mean. They lost three of their children, one to malaria and two to . . . well, two were shot. Nothing seems important after that.

– But surely their remaining children are?

– I suppose so, David admitted.

As David Malwai gave him the address, which was on the edge of town, a new and not very fancy development where trees had not yet been planted and where the houses stood ungraced by foliage beneath the sky, Austin found himself weeping for no reason he could discern – something to do with the weight of his own mania, but also for Miriam's dead brothers. He gave a choked farewell to David and rang off.

• •

David presented himself at the Norths' house about seven p.m. on Friday. Meredith had never met him and was obviously impressed by his tall grace, the delicacy of his handshake and his compliments for their house, which was one of the finer ones in the street, an old Federation bungalow with sprawling verandahs, a house that should have been sufficient to keep a man content.

– We won't be too long, said Austin as they left.

In a peculiar state of fear and exultation, Austin drove himself and David past the library, the shire offices where Meredith was queen of the sporting ovals and playgrounds, and turned left at the RSL. Its bowling club lawns stood flat, immaculate and sterile under the low sky.

They reached the outskirts of town and, at David's instruction, pulled up before a brick-veneer house like all the others around it. David led Austin through a comfortless front garden to the door.

There was no bell and the engineer knocked. Austin heard mysterious noises within, and a cry or two. The door was thrown open and the breath of the house, the pungent combinations of the meal now eaten, broke over him. Austin saw a tall, gnarled man with ceremonial scars along his cheeks, two either side. A displaced warrior.

– Mr Salong, said David, holding out his hand. May I introduce one of Miriam's teachers, Mr Austin North.

The big man shook Austin's hand, frowning and with those suspicious eyes he had seen from Miriam's direction. Mr Salong gestured them towards the dim corridor that led into the house. These rites of welcome, Austin North felt with a genuine compassion, might be ones he would have learned as a child, then had shocked out of him by events, and which he was now redeploying. For there was a certain creakiness to them.

Down the corridor, they came to the lounge room. Unlike most lounge rooms there was no TV set casting its radiance on the family's faces. There were no pictures on the walls, either – they had not settled on which images they wanted or were entitled to by their new existence here.

Staring at Austin with the same stark, handsome features she had given to her daughter, the mother in her long white gown and drawn-back hood sat on the main lounge. She did not rise or extend a hand to Austin or David, though she nodded vigorously to David and yielded a momentary half-smile. Beside her, bare-footed and in her long school uniform, sat Miriam, wearing the shy smile of a girl whose family house is suddenly discovered by her teacher. On single chairs waited two brothers in the uniform of the local Catholic school. They were upright and formal.

The father and mother both signalled Austin towards the chair he should take – one of the boys was sitting on a kitchen chair to make it possible for Austin to have the seat of honour and greater comfort, like the one the father occupied across the room. David Malwai took a seat in a slightly less distinguished bit of furniture. He nodded to all the family, and wished them peace in Arabic.

The father murmured *chai* and the mother assented, nodding.

– *Chai.*

At once Miriam rose and left the room. In her absence, David Malwai started speaking to the parents, either in Arabic or in Dinka, their native language. He pointed to and smiled at Austin, and Austin nodded to the parents again and watched for Miriam's return. The parents sat impassively, the upright father with his hands on his knees. But although Austin could not read them, as the big man suddenly turned his eyes in his direction, Austin wondered whether he was being read, and if his condition of half-joy and self-reproach was being weighed up by Mr Salong.

At last David turned to Austin.

– I have been telling them about Miriam's running and about how hard it is for her to run in her school tunic. In a moment I shall show them the picture.

David Malwai took the photograph from his pocket, but before he could rise and show it to Mr Salong, Miriam glided into the room, bearing a tin tray with seven glasses on it full of tea, and a big sugar bowl.

– Do you want sugar? David Malwai asked.

– No thank you, said Austin. David Malwai spoke to Miriam and she repeated to her parents what Austin had said. It seemed to cause astonishment to the family that anyone should drink *chai* without sugar. But Miriam brought the glass to him and set it down on a side table by his chair. He picked it up but did not drink yet. The tea inside the tumbler burned his hands, but he would not put down this offered token. David Malwai took plenty of sugar in his glass, thereby not causing cultural amazement amongst the Salongs.

Next Miriam, her head slightly lowered, spooned sugar into a glass of the scalding tea for her father and presented it to him, then a glass each to her mother and brothers – they all seemed to have asbestos fingers – and then sugared her own and lifted the glass and went to sit down again beside her mother.

– We'll just talk for a while now, David Malwai told Austin. He implied he would show the Salongs the picture once the tea was drunk. Tea drinking was obviously a serious rite with them.

– Well . . . perhaps you could tell them their daughter is doing very well, said Austin.

David Malwai translated this and the parents nodded sagely. Slowly people finished their tea – since they drank it while it was still so hot, Austin preferred to blister his throat than be far behind them. The father and then the mother reached out and put their glasses down on the tray on the central table. So did the boys, to whom the father muttered something and who now vanished from the room. David Malwai finished and reached for Austin's glass. Austin thought for a panicked second he might have to leave due to his scalded throat.

But now they would descend to business. David Malwai crossed to the father and handed him the picture of Megan Wishart. He explained items of the clothing to them and occasionally nodded in Austin's direction. What would the idea of winning races, of regional or state high school championships, even of national titles and world cups and Olympics, mean to them, to whom speed and endurance had chiefly counted for escape?

The father studied the photograph closely. Then he rose from his own chair and formally sat on the main settee beside his wife, and there they were, three sculptured people, the father rough-hewn of granite, the mother of warmer stone, Miriam of lustrous black marble.

Miriam had not presumed to look at the photograph her parents were weighing. It was not her business. She gathered the tray of glasses and left with them. David Malwai kept speaking reassuringly. Austin was sure David knew it would be a good thing for the Salongs, for the Sudanese community. He knew, as the Salongs didn't, that the Australians measured themselves by sport and conceded respect to immigrant races chiefly in terms of sport. The mother murmured at length to the husband. Austin hoped Miriam might come back and exercise the sort of power teenage girls seemed so accomplished at in most of Australia. Mr Salong began speaking in his measured, sonorous way. When he'd finished he looked straight ahead. With a diplomatic delicacy, his neat hands on his knees, David Malwai turned to Austin.

– They've decided against it, he told Austin. They said they permit her to wear a school uniform only because it is customary here. You understand how it is? The Coptic Christians have a code of modesty and they fear nakedness. Mr Salong says that's what the animists do.

Miriam's father rose, crossed the floor and gave the picture back to David Malwai, who in turn passed it to Austin. At this moment Miriam walked back into the room in that long school tunic, passed her father and mother, and then turned and sat at her mother's side. The mother reached out her arm, and Miriam lifted her feet from the floor, tucked them beneath her, and lowered her head in a gesture of utter acceptance onto her mother's breast, as if it were the source of a beloved authority. It was as if she were listening for affirmation from her mother's heart. The submissive embrace was something his own daughter – however fine a kid – would not have extended to Meredith. Most girls would have thought it too uncool, surrendering too much ground in their contest with their mothers as to who would rule.

And watching that gesture, that obeisance, Austin saw Miriam's childhood laid bare to him and found himself in a second humiliated and cured. The heart to which Miriam now listened was the constant clock in the world of flux which had brought her at last here, to this bare suburb, and into his classroom. And seeing Miriam resort this way, with such bodily grace, to the one given of her universe, he saw himself with acute pain as simply another predator, as one with the soldiers and militias who came storming in, maiming and demeaning, carrying off cattle and burning the grain. His obsession had reduced him to the role of just another plunderer.

Though instantly reborn, he could tell at once that he was somehow a diminished man, frightened, cured but suffering the most bitter doubt about what he had not doubted before – his effectuality on earth, his equilibrium as a friend to humankind, a friend of poetry, an acquaintance of history.

– Please tell Mr and Mrs Salong that I understand, he said.

He wanted to run. But as had happened with the boy Grice, he couldn't shut up.

– Perhaps you could assure them we wish Miriam no harm. But we accept totally their authority.

Shut up, Austin, he told himself.

David Malwai delivered the message. The mother and father made gracious sounds and nodded to Austin. Miriam raised her head and smiled at Austin.

Out in the cold car again, waiting for the heating to kick in, David Malwai said, They might come round. They don't mind her running.

Austin realised that Miriam, whose English was so good, must have understood a great deal of the conversation. She had kept silent in the parental debate. No pleading, no whining, no challenge had broken her settled surface.

• •

The following morning he wanted to hide at home and go anywhere but to the high school.

– You look tired, said Meredith.

– I think I'm getting sick of teaching, he said. Do you have any openings for gardeners and groundsmen?

– You're joking, aren't you? asked Meredith.

– If an opening comes up, honest, let me know.

– You *are* serious.

He was all right while he was actually in class. It was between classes that shame and self-knowledge corroded him. He was aware he was not the sociable man he once was, and his colleagues, he could see, were bemused by this. Meredith was bemused too, and his daughter frowned. Where had her predictably grinning, out-of-date father gone?

In the autumn, in secret and at Meredith's insistence, he visited one of the town's two psychiatrists. The psychiatrist said it was a matter of serotonin, a neural transmitter the body made less of as one hit middle-age.

The last issue of the news bulletin for the year was a large one with reproduced photographs. There was a picture of Miriam, wearing the sort of running gear Megan Wishart had – breaking the fifteen hundred–metre record for the New South Wales Open Schoolgirls Final. In an echo of previous times, she smashed it by 4.7 seconds.

7

Twelve Minutes

Melina Marchetta

I

2005

To: tomfmackee@hotmail.com

From: joemackee@yahoo.com

Sent: 28th June, 2005

Subject: Nothing Comes of Nothing

My delusional, numb-skulled nephew.

How long is this going to go on, mate? The obsession with this girl whose name you haven't stopped saying since you were sixteen. Conquer this passion. Do something about it! Yeats it, Tom. STD.

My advice? Get out the Norton's poetry anthology I left you, and you better bloody still have it, because if you lost it like you did my Slade Alive LP, I will hunt you down, son. Page 1902. *Japan*. Not about the Japanese, but about moments of perfection. Commit it to memory and you make good use of it. Because if I come home and you're still pining over this little girl without having given her a chance, I will call you a chicken shit for the rest of your life. C.S. Tom, for short.

And can you please clear your crap out of Georgie's attic. She reckons you use her place like it's a hotel. Don't expect me to bring my girl to a hovel.

With much love and affection

Joe.

PS. Tell your father to get stuffed about the roosters getting beaten by the tigers. One text message a day is enough to gloat.

Tom googles Yeats and works out that STD is all about seizing the day and not some sexually transmitted disease. He knew that all along, he'll tell his uncle, Mr Expert on dishing out advice about footy and women. He's curious to know if Joe works out the subject line before he begins the email or after. Joe's an English teacher so everything has a theme. Most times it's the Shakespeare he's teaching. Tom can tell it's *King Lear* these days. Last week's subject line was 'Poor Tom's a Cold', just because he wrote to complain about the wind-chill factor at Brookvale oval.

In the kitchen, his mum is stuffing some fruit and a muesli bar in her lunch bag and peering out the back window.

'Check your father out,' she says.

Tom stands beside her, the morning light blinding him for a moment as he watches his dad hunch over the timber.

'He pencils a line,' she explains, still intrigued after all these years, 'and then he stands back for hours thinking about whether it's right or not. Next he's going to run his fingers along the timber and if there's one little splinter out of place, he'll file it back. With my nail file, mind you. *Prick.*'

But it's an insult laced with affection. She picks up her satchel and kisses Tom's cheek.

'Tell him it's time to go to work and that we've got Annie's confirmation talks tonight and don't forget to move your crap out of Georgie's attic, Tom. You know she wants to get things ready for Joe.' She knocks at the window and holds up a hand in a wave and then she's off. She's wearing 'the outfit' today, which means her office is in talks with useless policy makers.

He pours cereal into a bowl with milk and walks out the back to watch the master at work. It's bloody freezing and he's regretting not putting on any clothes except for the boxers.

'You're going to be late,' he yawns. On the bench is a good slab of timber, a river red gum. His father's making a table for Nanni Grace for when Joe and his girl come to visit from London.

'Straddle it, will you,' his dad says, grabbing hold of the electric saw. 'Hold it still.'

Tom's not happy with the suggestion. 'You better not get that too close to you-know-where,' he mutters, swallowing a mouthful of cornflakes and putting down the bowl.

His father stares at a spot he missed and begins filing again before he puts on his goggles and switches on the saw. When it's over, Tom's shaking his head with disbelief, pointing to his private parts. His father's grinning.

He's looking good, Tom thinks. There was a time, a couple of years back, when his old man was heading towards some kind of meltdown, courtesy of too many liquid lunches and union negotiations between hostile employers and the disgruntled employees of the world. But forty was looking good on him. 'It's the new thirty,' his Aunt Georgie said when she and his dad had their joint party.

His father takes off the goggles. 'Listen,' he says, 'Georgie wants you to—'

'I know,' Tom interrupts. 'She wants me to get my shit out of her attic. You'd think a king was returning the way she's going on.'

His dad shrugs. 'He's her little brother. You know how she is about Joe.'

'Like you're not,' Tom scoffs. 'His woman's going to be with him, you know, and he's not going to be able to do all the shit you've got planned. Can't imagine Penelope Cruz at the footy or at the pub every night.' They call her that because she's Spanish. Georgie calls her Pen for short.

His dad lifts his arm to stretch a muscle and Tom reaches over and pokes him in the gut.

'What's this? Looks like flab, Dominic.'

Tom loves calling him that too, just to piss him off.

'Little shit,' his father says, holding his gut in and slapping his abs. 'Watch this body. It's what yours'll look like one day.'

'Mum noticed it from the kitchen,' Tom lies, grinning. 'She's like, "Check out that carcass, will ya!"'

Before he can duck, his father hooks him around the neck with his elbow and they both struggle for a while. It's allowed to get as vicious as they want without any repercussions, and these days it's the only physical contact they have with each other. They're both killing themselves laughing and neither gives in. Tom's got the upper hand, but he knows he can lose it any moment now.

'She didn't seem to have a problem with it last night,' his father manages between grunts when they've both hit the ground.

Tom shoves him back and tries not to choke at the idea of whatever his parents got up to the night before. He's just been given a reason to be in counselling for the rest of his life.

Later, they carry the slab of timber onto the grass. He can tell the table's going to be beautiful and he can understand his father's obsession with getting it right. They both stare at it for a moment. The smell of it, mingled with the silky oak and lavender in the backyard, makes him smile.

'Nice,' Tom says.

'Getting there.'

'Can I borrow fifty bucks?'

He gets the look.

Tom laughs. 'I can't fit a job in between band and uni and they pay shit for gigs these days.'

'What about the contacts your mum had?' his dad asks.

'Rang and spoke to four very polite computers who gave me all these options and then cut out on me. Then I tried the post office, because they were advertising, and I spoke to another computer. Very rude, that one. Don't think it recognised "Are you shitting me?" as an option.'

'You know why that is?'

'Why is that, Dominic?' he asks, drolly, because he knows he's going to be told why.

'Because we don't live in a society anymore, Tom. We live in an economy. We're not citizens. We're customers. That's what this government's done to us.'

'Can't I just ask you for fifty bucks and you be Marcel Marceau?'

His father, the smart arse, mimes out the handing of the money and they're both grinning again.

'As long as I don't have to chase you to pay it back.' He looks at Tom suspiciously. 'What's it for?'

'Membership for the Young Libs.'

'Very fucking funny.'

Tom grins. 'I'm wooing a girl.'

• •

There are a thousand things about her that turn Tom on. There's the lopsided way she walks because of the satchel of books that weighs her down, and there's the fringe that covers her eyes, and no matter how many times he's looked into them, he can't tell if they're green or brown, just somewhere in between. She told him the day before that one of the girls had convinced her to do stuff with her hair. Foils she called them, and he didn't understand foils so she showed him using alfoil and he thought *how bloody stupid*, until he sees what the foils do to her hair now, all gold-like mixed with the brown and the way it's cut jagged around her chin makes her look scruffy one minute and cool the next, and he begins to strum the guitar and starts crooning 'Danke Schoen' because he knows she likes it from watching *Ferris Bueller* so many times and then she's smiling and laughing and yes, Joe, it's time to STD.

'Plans?' she asks, but she's talking to Francesca and Justine, who are packing up behind him. She could be avoiding him. Things flared up between them again this week. It amazes him how they can go for ages being best mates and just hanging out to eye contact that lasts just a tad too long, turning their relationship into all things confusing. Last time it happened was two years ago on graduation night when the gang ended up at Maroubra Beach with their dates. That night he couldn't keep his eyes off her, despite the fact that he was there with one of the year eleven girls and she had decided to go it alone. They drove around the city with Tom as their designated driver, planning to stay the night on the beach, where there was too much drinking and too much emotion between all of them. And he remembered the water and how warm it felt and one of the guys doing a nudie run along the beach, and then they all stripped down to underwear and in the darkness he knew exactly where to find her, hadn't realised he was looking until his hand snaked out and grabbed her, their mouths connecting and tongues taking over while his brain was saying *danger danger will robinson*.

• •

And then there was last Monday, when they were watching a band at the Sando with some of his mates from uni. He had stood behind her with his arms around her and his chin resting on the top of her head. Nothing new about that. They were a tactile bunch, all of them. But she leaned back to say something and that was it. Again. And he couldn't let go. Not when they were sitting at the Buzz Bar in Newtown having a hot chocolate: his hands were playing with hers and she let them play and then they were crossing King Street to go back to one of the guys' houses in Erskineville and he was holding her hand and she let him and he knew that if he tried to kiss her, she'd let him. But he didn't.

He was never a coward when it came to girls.

But this was Tara Finke.

'Will and I are going to Sallo's party down at Cockle Bay so come with us,' Francesca says.

'She's not dressed for it,' Tom points out. Tara's wearing a skirt over jeans and some high-neck black skivvy that flattens her even more than she is, but it's not nightclub stuff and he's cheering in silence.

'Come to my gig,' Justine says, locking the case of her accordion. 'It's just a bit of a jam session with some of the guys at the Con.'

'Will I be the only who's not a musical genius?' Tara asks.

'Probably,' Tom answers for Justine. 'And it'll make you feel inferior and then depressed and you'll want to slit your wrists and you don't want to be caught dead wearing a skirt over jeans. I mean, what is that look, Finke? Really? On the other hand, I'm cleaning my stuff out of Georgie's attic so you may as well come with me.'

He says it pretty blasé and shrug-like.

'Oh the choices,' she sighs, unravelling herself from her satchel and putting it down on the floor. 'I've got to go to the loo.'

He watches her walk away and the skirt rides up her jeans and sits where he wants it to sit and although there's no flesh showing, his body has already kick-started into something completely out of his control. He feels Justine and Francesca come up beside him and he puts an arm around both of them, humming 'Danke Schoen' until he realises they aren't just standing around waiting. They're staring up at him.

He looks from one to the other. 'What?' he asks, on the defensive. '*What*?'

'What are you doing?' Francesca asks.

'Thomas?' This from Justine, who usually protects him from the wrath of the other girls.

His hands fall to his side.

'What did I do now?'

'Do you want us to fill you in on something, Tom,' Francesca asks, Queen of Rhetorical Questions, because she's going to fill him in whether he wants to be filled in or not. 'You know how Siobhan gave Tara a mobile phone for her birthday. Well we set it up for her so that every time one of us rings, a particular tune comes on. Have you heard of Tom Petty and the Heartbreakers, Tom? Because when you ring her, the tune "Stop Dragging My Heart Around" comes on.'

Now he's really pissed. '*Back*,' he says, looking at Justine. '*Off*,' he says to Francesca.

'I'm texting Siobhan,' she says, referring to Tara's best friend who is working in London.

He looks at them both with disbelief. 'As if I'm scared of Siobhan.'

Francesca gets out her phone and in desperation he grabs it from her.

'Please, Frankie. I'm begging. Don't text Siobhan.'

Tara walks back into the hall and Francesca manages to pry her phone out of his fingers by giving him one of those pinches where she grips the hair on his arm and twists.

He grabs his guitar and jumps off the stage, picking up Tara's satchel and steering her towards the door.

'I haven't said goodbye to them,' she says, trying to get her satchel from him. He slings it over his neck.

'Tara says bye,' he calls over his shoulder.

• •

'I like the alfoils.'

'Foils, fool,' she says, wiggling her fingers to a kid who's sitting opposite them on the bus. Somewhere back in year twelve the insults became signs of affection.

She's tired and leans her head on his shoulder, which is the resting place for all their heads, but when Justine and Siobhan and Francesca use his body so shamelessly he doesn't feel the need to turn his head and press his mouth against their hair.

'I've finally decided about the Masters,' she says. 'Perma-culture.'

'Hmm, Permaculture.'

She's looking at him. 'You don't even know what it means.'

'Yeah, I do. It's a hair thing. Like the alfoils.'

'You're a dick.' But she laughs all the same. 'It works perfectly with Cultural Studies. There's a component of overseas study, so I'm going to look at how we can create a sustainable urban environment.'

'Huh?'

He feels her watching him and when he shifts his eyes to look down into hers, she's staring intently.

'Do you know what I'm talking about?'

He sighs. He knows exactly what she's talking about. He doesn't mind the sustainable or the urban or the environment. It's the word 'overseas' he doesn't care to dwell on.

A bunch of gigglers vacate the back seat at Central and Tom grabs both their stuff and leads.

'And I owe it all to your great Aunt Margie,' she says, settling into the corner.

Oh yeah, thank you, Great Auntie Margie. Love your work.

'She introduced me to one of the nuns. You remember her? Sister Josephine. When she spoke about East Timor at the Town Hall a couple of years back? Well, we've been emailing and she reckons I should go over to Timor as part of my MA.'

He doesn't respond. Just looks past her, through the window, as if construction on Broadway is mesmerising.

'You're not interested in what I'm doing,' she says, her voice flat.

He moves away from her so he can look at her properly.

'No, I'm not interested,' he says, pissed off.

Her face goes instantly pink. She's in retreat and it's going to take him forever to force her back into advance. That's Tara Finke for you. The moment she stops making speeches and proving a point, the rhetoric goes flying out the window and she's all awkwardness, stuck to a wall of vulnerability built over the years. Tom can get her off that wall.

'You're going overseas for how long?' he asks.

'Forget it. You're not interested, remember?'

Now she's peering outside. Glebe Point Road's never looked this exciting. He can't keep his eyes off her and he knows she feels it no matter how hard she's looking out that window. Because her face deepens in colour until he actually thinks she's going to cry.

'What part of you going overseas, for probably more than a year, would you like me to be excited about?' he snaps. There's no turning back now. She looks up and he can see it in her eyes. She gets what he's saying. Her face is flushed again. A different kind of flush.

'Go out to Campbelltown, Tara. They've got a bigger need for ecological design out there.'

She smiles. 'You do know what it means, you moron?'

He leans closer, his mouth an inch away from hers. 'Not working against nature,' he says, 'working with nature.'

She's looking at his mouth and then up at his eyes.

'That's what permaculture means,' he says with a grin.

She laughs and leans her head back against him.

'I've never even been on a plane, you know. The only place I've been to is my grandparents' house at The Entrance.'

'A very underestimated part of the world, The Entrance is.'

Each time the bus door opens he feels a blast of cold air. When she shivers he puts his arm around her. Should have kissed her a moment ago when the time was right.

'So you email my great aunt?'

'She reckons you and your dad are going out to Walgett to build something out there,' she says.

'Does she now? Can think of a thousand better ways of spending my holidays, but you know my father. Gets anal about things, so it's going to be Tom and Dom's excellent adventures in Walgett.'

'Fun times?'

'Reckons he's going to convince my Uncle Joe to come along while he's out here from London, which'll mean that my step-pop's going to want to come too and it'll be the Mackee men building the world, while trying not to get into punch-ups after a couple of schooners.'

He grins. He doesn't realise he kind of likes the sound of that.

By the time they get off at Stanmore they've tackled everything from the United Nations to Brad and Angelina, and it's while he's doing *Little Britain* impersonations and she's wheezing from laughing that he stops and leans down to kiss her. Her satchel is a barrier between them and when he tries to put an arm around her, his guitar case batters her side and she almost goes flying out onto the road. He has only one free hand to hold her, and it just seems to be his mouth pressing down on hers and Tara on tip-toes trying to reach him. And by the time they reach Georgie's house they've stopped four times and he just wants to get her into the house and up in the attic where his junk can stay another day. It's late and he figures that Georgie is sleeping, but as they creep up the stairs she comes out of her room.

'Yes we are cleaning out the Messiah's room,' he says, casually. Georgie points to her cheek and he kisses her, and although she says nothing there's that close scrutiny of hers which kind of says everything.

He mumbles something about going upstairs and continues as if every part of him isn't trembling, and as if his head is not screaming, *Georgie knows you want to have sex with Tara Finke tonight under her roof!* Tara stays behind and he can hear them talk about her mum, who's just left the Red Cross to work for the Cancer Council and about a job vacancy that Georgie should look into. But then Tara's there in the attic and he shuts the door behind her.

'What's that?' she asks, looking down at the LP in his hands and he knows she's nervous and stalling.

'Slade. I'm going to paste it up on the wall so my dickhead uncle sees it the moment he walks in and stops going on about me losing it.'

His stuff is scattered all over the floor.

'You're such a slob.'

But then they're kissing again and he's unbuttoning her jeans and she's shaking.

'Stop shaking,' he whispers.

'Georgie knows. I can tell she knows. And I've never noticed how beautiful she is. Like one of those actresses from the 1940s, all dark hair and white skin. No freckles. How did she get to have that colour skin with no freckles?'

'You're babbling, Finke.'

And she's wearing too many clothes. Jeans, skirt and probably, under it all, tights.

He bends and pulls down her jeans first. 'How short is this skirt?' he says with wonder. No tights.

'It's why I wear the jeans. Siobhan gave it to me.'

'How white are these legs?' he says with more wonder. Goosebumped to the hilt. He runs his fingers over them. When he stands up again he pulls off his jumper. She's still shaking.

'You've got to stop shaking, Tara,' he says gently. 'It's just me.'

'I can't do this if Georgie's downstairs, Tom. It'll be like having my mother there.'

He tries to take off her top but she's shaking her head emphatically. 'With the light off.'

'No light off,' he argues. 'I want to see you.'

And it's a bit of fear he sees on her face and he doesn't want that between them, so he reaches over and switches off the light and then takes her hand.

'We'll lie down. I promise. We won't do anything you don't want to do.'

Please please say we can do anything you want to do, Tom.

'It's just, if Georgie wasn't downstairs . . .'

And he's holding her to him and then they're underneath the blankets and she's trembling and he wants it to stop and for her to go back to being the Tara in charge and bossy so he won't have to deal with this vulnerability. The skirt is still on, but it barely covers her and he presses his knee between her legs.

'Come on, baby girl,' he whispers.

She stiffens. 'Don't call me baby girl!'

'Okay, honey.' He can just imagine the look on her face but can't see it in the dark. 'No? Bunny? Sweet cheeks? Babe? Darlin' chicky babe? Munchkin? Poppet?'

And she's doing that wheezing laugh again.

'Doll? Treasure?'

'Enough.'

'Petal.'

He kisses her again because he can't stop.

'Okay,' he sighs. 'I've just got to go somewhere. I'll be back in a minute.'

'Where?' she asks, alarmed. And then he's crawling under the sheets and he's peeling her undies from her and he loves that they're lace and cotton and he loves the smell of her and he wants to be all poetic but in an instant he forgets Joe's poem about Japan except the part about *you are the bell and I am the tongue ringing you* and a new sound enters his life, like when he was a kid and he first heard the sound of horse hooves clip-clopping and he asked his mother in wonder, 'What's that sound because I've never heard it before?' because now he hears the sound Tara Finke makes because of what *he's* doing to her and it's a good sound, a great one and he has no idea why he's thinking of horses and stuff, but he wants to hear that type of music for the rest of his life.

When he's up beside her again and when he thinks he's going to burst from wanting, he rests on his elbows looking down at her.

'Am I heavy?'

'No. Yes.'

'I thought you were getting all religious on me with your "Oh Gods".'

He lies back and she rests her head on his chest and then she looks up at him and he can feel her breath on his adam's apple.

'Tell me if I'm doing it wrong,' she whispers and he feels her hand crawl down his boxers and he wants to warn her, because she's not prepared for what's about to happen. And then she starts *talking*.

'My mum and dad —'

'No no no no no,' he gasps. 'You can't bring up your mum and dad while your hand is down there, Finke.'

And her tongue comes out and licks his throat.

'They're going to The Entrance next weekend,' she says. 'Such an underestimated place. And I can't go because I've got exams. So there'll be no one else in the house. No one downstairs.'

And then he gets all religious on her.

Later, when they're almost asleep, he calls out to her.

'Finke?'

'Yeah?'

'We'll make a good team. You plant. I build.'

• •

To: tomfmackee@hotmail.com

From: joemackee@yahoo.com

Sent: 1 July, 2005

Subject: Nothing Comes of Nothing Part 2

Damn, Tom. I don't know what kind of advice to give you from here. Make sure you know where it's going because you've become a bit of a tomcat when it comes to the opposite sex, and this girl doesn't seem the type who plays your games.

It's all a bit of a gamble, mate. That's all I can promise you. And we never get to see what that other life would have looked like if we don't take chances. You know what I did on the day before I started at this job? A practice run on the Tube from Covent Garden to Arsenal. I was miserable, Joe, sitting on the train, homesick for you all, honestly thinking of packing my shit up and flying back to Georgie's place and meditating in her attic for the rest of my life. I'd been here for almost six months and nothing had happened. And I was praying, Tom. I was praying for a sign. I was so close to being a no-show the next day. But thank God I went through with it because every day, now, I sit on the Tube and think I almost missed out. Just say I didn't know I was twelve minutes away from the rest of my life. Twelve minutes away from meeting a bunch of the most decent kids I'll ever teach. Twelve minutes away from meeting my girl.

Anyways, enough of this sentimental crap. Just do the right thing. Don't be a little man, Tom Thumb. Give a kiss to Annabel. Why is it that the sanest member of our family is a twelve-year-old? She played me the last post on the trumpet over the phone the other day and I fucking bawled my eyes out.

See you in twenty-three days for the great Finch and Mackee reunion. Can't wait. And I mean that.

Love

Joe

II
2007

He decides to walk home from the hospital. It's dark outside but Tom can't see the time on the clock of his phone because the glass face has cracked, no doubt at the same time as his head hit the table. He rings the landline at the flat but a recorded message on his phone warns him that he's almost out of credit so he hangs up before the answering machine sucks up what's left. He has a hazy recollection of having topped up his phone card and can't for the life of him remember where it's all gone, but nothing seems to be making sense to him at the moment. He stops twice from the dizziness and sits on the brick fence that lines the hospital on Missenden Road and watches an ambulance drive in and offload some drunk they've probably picked up off the streets. Six blocks east of the home he grew up in and Tom feels as if he's the last man on earth.

He swears he's just heard Tara Finke's voice for the first time in almost two years. *Talk to me, Tom. Just talk to me.* But if he's going to dream up any words from her, they'd be angry ones. Not ones said with such empathy. Maybe it's the concussion, or the morphine wearing off from the stitches on his face that makes him think of her. He knows she's got a boyfriend over there in Timor. That much he's got out of Francesca and Justine. These days his contact with the girls is limited to the once or twice a week they cross each other's path at The Union, one of those incestuous inner west things where everyone ends up drinking or working at the same pub. And you know how it happens. One day you pass strangers by and think, *I used to hang out with them*. But that was a world before dropping out of uni and parents splitting and one-night stands with a girl whose name you can't get out of your head and favourite uncles who used to call you Tom Thumb being blown to smithereens on their way to work on the other side of the world.

Some day he'd like to explain it to the girls. What he saw in their eyes that made him want to tell them to fuck off. Compassion. Empathy. It's a killer. It disarms you when you least want to be disarmed. Back then, tears constantly welled up in their eyes. 'How are you, Tom?' they'd ask. It's what he has been able to tolerate about living with his flatmates this past year. They drink, they smoke their weed, they play their music and the days pass in a haze where nobody analyses how he feels, how he's supposed to feel, how he'll feel the next day, how he feels about the present which is shaped by the past and can impact on the future. With his flatmates, Tom just exists. Except merely existing doesn't seem to be enough these days. Because tonight, when Tom's face was heading for that glass table, he had fantasised about how good the pain would feel on impact, and then when he woke up in that hospital bed, every voice he had blocked out for eighteen months crowded his head. Tara Finke's. Joe's. Even his Aunt Georgie's. It was like he had been etherised for eighteen months and now he could feel every sensation, hear every voice.

• •

Later that week, he goes to see his Aunt Georgie. Hasn't been by for ages. Sometimes, when he does, they sit outside on the front step. He can't stomach going inside. Too many memories. Today, she stares at the stitches around his eye and he lets her touch them and he wants to weep at the feel of her fingers. She's told him before that if he gets his shit together, he can move back in with her. Save a bit of money, maybe go back to uni. Keep each other company. She tries to talk to him about his father, but he puts up a hand and blocks her. He'll talk about anything. He'll even talk about Joe. But not his father.

She tells him to ring his mother and sister because they miss him like hell but all Tom can think of is that last time he saw his mum was when she had visited for a weekend to convince him to come up to Brisbane where she had taken his sister to stay with his grandparents. He was stoned out of his brain that day, staring right through her the whole time. But he wasn't stoned enough to forget the look on her face. He'll take that look to his grave.

He tries to explain to Georgie how he's feeling. 'It's grief, Tom,' Georgie says on the step beside him.

'But it's been almost two years.'

She looks at him confused, the circles under her eyes so dark. 'Did someone promise you there was a time limit?'

He needs to believe there is, because he can't go on feeling like this for the rest of his life.

She touches his face again and smiles. 'When you rang me the other night, I thought that maybe you were ready to come back now.'

He stares at her, shaking his head.

'I didn't ring you.'

'On the night you did this to yourself,' she says touching his stitches again. 'We spoke about your father. You said you wanted to finish the table Dominic was making for Nanni Grace.'

He wonders what else he's blocked from that night.

At the mention of his father's name again he asks the question. 'Do you know where he is?'

Doesn't know why. Before she responds, he walks away, down the steps and out onto the street. It's what Tom does. He asks the questions, but walks away from the answers.

He's always enjoyed being a coward like that.

Except he's not even halfway home when he realises the truth and it makes him feel sick to his gut. With trembling fingers he takes the phone out of his pocket and goes to the call log, backtracking to three nights ago.

Talk to me, Tom. Just talk to me.

And there are the names. Tara Finke. Right above

Georgie's. *Fuck*, right below Joe's. He was a busy boy that night, ringing up ghost after ghost. God knows what he said. To Georgie he promised to build a table. And Tara? What the hell did he say to Tara? He wonders if he can live with the unknown. Does he leave it and never find out what he said to her three nights ago or does he just ring her so she can reveal to him, in full colourful detail, the fucking idiot fool he made of himself. He decides against. And then for. And then against.

He makes it to midnight before it swings back to 'for'.

'Hey.' His voice feels croaky and he can hear her breathing on the other side.

Then silence.

'When I rang you this week, what did I say?' he asks.

'Nothing,' she says. Her voice makes him ache.

'No really. I need to know.'

He's begging God that he didn't make a fool of himself. Not with her.

'I didn't declare my love for you or anything like that?' he asks in a ridiculous jocular voice.

'No.'

Relief.

'So I rang and said nothing?'

'Nothing at all, Tom.' Her voice is flat. Disappointed. There's no surprise at him ringing again for the second time this week after not hearing from him for eighteen months.

He can sense she's about to say something and it seems like hours rather than seconds before he asks again.

'Nothing? Are you sure?'

He wants to ask her what made her say the words *Talk to me, Tom. Talk to me.*

'You cried,' she says, her voice so gentle it kills him. Tara Finke doesn't do gentle. Tara Finke does practical or abrupt or furious or passionate. But the gentleness in her voice undoes him. 'That's all. You just cried.'

'Sorry,' he mutters. 'Shit, I'm sorry.'

'You should be sorry for other things, Tom. Not crying because you're sad.'

And then he can't help himself, because he's a prick like that. Can't help asking her the question.

'Do you remember that night we were in your house? Because I can't get it out of my head.'

She hangs up.

• •

He sends her an email per day. He's written to her before, but she's never responded. But he has to believe that things are different because she didn't have to answer her phone both times and she did. He sends her links to their past. He sends her updates of his day. He sends her the question he asked on the phone. And then one day he sees the address in his inbox.

tarajfinke@yahoo.com

Dear Tom

I'll tell you what I remember, seeing you asked. I remember that after we made love you asked me to get out of bed, naked. I mean we had just had sex, so that's as intimate as I thought it got, but it's funny that I don't remember that part as much as I remember you making me stand in front of you with nothing on and we were freezing cold and I felt so exposed, like I felt you could see inside the guts of me. And remember, I cried? And you were like, *Shh Shh, don't. You're beautiful*, and I can't believe I'm writing this now, remembering it, but I don't think I'll ever forget your voice when you said that.

But then Joe happened, and you didn't ring or anything. You didn't let me see you exposed from all your pain, Tom. You hid and you left me there, starkers, and for so long, *for so so long*, I felt raw. Don't ever ask anyone to do that again, Tom. Don't ever ask them to bare their soul and then leave it. It's fucking cruel and no matter how much pain you were in, you had no right to do that to me. Because sometimes it makes me want to shudder, because sometimes I still think I'm there in my bedroom standing naked, except it's like the whole world can see me, and they're laughing. And it makes me just want to cry with shame.

She'll call this closure. Her opportunity to say what she's always wanted said. He'll respect the fact that she won't want a response to keep things alive. She'll want this dead and finished, so he'll log off on that part of his life. He looks at her name one more time. Reads her email one more time. Tells himself to log off one more time. Except there it is. In his inbox from eighteen months before.

From: joemackee@yahoo.com

Subject: Nothing Comes of Nothing

The one his uncle sent the morning when life was so fucking perfect and his father was in the backyard crafting a table for the whole Mackee family to fit around instead of drinking himself into some kind of oblivion. When his mum and Annabel lived in Sydney and Tom was one step away from getting it right with the girl he'd been in love with since year eleven.

And somehow Tom knows that he has to start somewhere. That he can't spend the rest of his days like someone out of the first sentence of a TS Eliot poem. Not this Tom.

He thinks maybe he'll step inside Georgie's house tonight and then take her out for a bite to eat.

Maybe he'll ring his mum. Write Annabel an email.

Maybe he'll stop hating his father for letting everything fall apart when he should have been the one to hold it together.

Nothing comes of nothing.

Maybe . . .

Dear Tara,

If you think I've forgotten anything about that night in your room, you, most gorgeous girl, are labouring under a great misapprehension. I remember everything. I remember your petticoat . . . slip . . . whatever the hell it's called, and how you let me take it off. You made me close my eyes and that was even more of a turn on.

But when Joe happened, I couldn't speak anymore. I think I was scared that you wouldn't be able to make the numbness go away because my mum and dad and Annabel couldn't. And I remember thinking, if Tara can't make it go away, I think I'll want to bring on oblivion. So I never gave you the chance to try.

I know I fucked up and I know you're happy with whoever you've been with over there. Probably some great guy who I'll hate because he treats you the way I should have. But I'm holding out here, Tara. Because I heard it in your voice that night I cracked open my head and I have to believe that something is still there for you. And I need you to know that you probably thought I wasn't listening when you used to talk about stuff, but I remember the speech you made in year twelve, about choosing worthwhile degrees and that you believed in trade, not aid and that the only way to stop poverty was to make people self-sufficient and I remember thinking, like I did that night in Georgie's attic, *I want to change the world with her*. That's a pretty powerful gift you have there, Ms Finke. To make the laziest guy around want to change the world because of you. So next time you remember standing in your bedroom naked, know that it is the most amazing view from any angle, especially the one where we get to see inside.

Love always

Always.

Tom

8

Manhattan Dreaming

Anita Heiss

When the director of the National Aboriginal Gallery calls you to her office, you go. And so I did, scurrying along the corridors of Old Parliament House, wondering what could possibly be so urgent. There'd been budget cuts, but my exhibition had already been locked in, so it couldn't be that. I hadn't been on MySpace to spy on Adam since the internet audit had been done, so it couldn't be that. I was so far ahead in programming that I was planning exhibitions for 2011, so I knew it wasn't my work performance. And yet I still felt sick with anxiety.

Emma was at her desk, about to make a call. When she saw me standing in the doorway she put the phone down. 'Hi, Lauren. Sit – I've got a proposition for you,' she said.

She waved a sheet of paper in front of my face. 'I've just received an email from the National Museum of the American Indian at the Smithsonian in New York City.

They've got a fellowship available for a visiting Indigenous curator.'

Emma was so excited she couldn't get her words out fast enough. 'The fellowship allows the chosen curator to work on their own *original* exhibition *and* curate within the museum generally.'

'Sounds interesting.'

'Interesting? Lauren, it's the chance of a lifetime for a young curator! I want to nominate *you* for it. I think you'd be perfect.' Emma smiled the hugest, widest grin, showing off her perfectly straight teeth.

'Me? But it's in New York. That's in America. And America is so far away, from *everything* and *everyone*!'

'I don't think you understand what I'm offering you,' Emma said. 'Seriously, this is a dream opportunity. You'd get the chance to network with other curators internationally and work with Native American artists from across the Americas.'

I put my hands on my chest to demonstrate my heartfelt appreciation. 'Emma, I'm so honoured you think I'm even up for the challenge. But what about my work here?'

'We both know that you're scheduling so far ahead I haven't even been allocated my budgets to cover the exhibitions you're planning in three years' time. I'm glad you're on top of everything, but I can afford to let you go right now – especially for something as important as this. I'm even happy to step in and help if need be while you're away – it's been a while since I did curatorial work, and to be honest I miss it.' She got up and walked over to straighten a Jimmy Pike painting on the wall. Then she stood back to admire it.

'It's really kind of you to think of me, but –'

Emma turned to face me. 'Look, I have to be upfront with you, Lauren. I'm not doing this entirely selflessly. I want to build a relationship between the Smithsonian and the NAG. We're a fledgling gallery and we need to build our profile internationally. You're the youngest senior curator in the Pacific, and having you on staff will get them – and us – heaps of publicity. Everyone wins.' She held both her palms out as if serving me the 'win' on a platter. Judging by the look on her face, she was seeking agreement from me.

'Everyone wins,' I repeated, not at all convinced.

'This fellowship would look sensational on your CV, Lauren.' Emma sat down again and eyeballed me across the desk. 'You'll be in a stronger position when you return to Australia having had this experience.'

I knew Emma was right, and she knew I wanted to go as far as possible in the art world, that I had my sights set on being the director of the NAG one day. But *I* knew I had plenty of time to work my way up the ranks, because Emma wasn't going anywhere for a while.

I moved to the edge of my seat and leant forward. 'I know it's a fantastic opportunity – it's just that – well, it's

America. I like it here, even with the miserable weather. It's my second home.'

'Firstly, Lauren, it's not forever – it's twelve months, with an option to extend for another year. And secondly, and most importantly, it's not just *anywhere* in America, it's New York. The Big Apple! Shopping on Fifth Avenue. Broadway shows. Times Square. Central Park. The Metropolitan Museum of Art and the Guggenheim. Doesn't any of that interest you?'

'To be honest, I like what's here. I'm not unhappy living in Canberra.' I had always felt I belonged in the ACT because my mob was all around me – in Canberra, Goulburn, Queanbeyan and just down the road in Wagga Wagga.

'*Not unhappy* and *happy* aren't quite the same thing, Lauren. But even if you're happy here, it doesn't mean you won't enjoy life in a big, bold, brilliant city', and she waved her arms around, 'like New York.'

'How do you think someone like me – Libby calls me a country bumpkin, you know – is going to survive in New York? A lone blackfella at that. This is big city enough for me. I was out of my depth in Sydney when I was studying.'

'But there's a whole world out there, Lauren!' She gave me that smile again. 'New York is an exciting place for a young single girl like you.'

Single. I had no real ties keeping me in Canberra now, even if I wished I did. Emma had no idea I'd been seeing

Adam, so she didn't know we'd broken up – or why, or how – but I felt like she'd knifed me in the heart.

'Before you make a decision I want you to give it some serious thought,' Emma said. 'I want you to know there is no one else I would even consider nominating. You're the best we have. And I don't say that lightly.'

She handed me the email. 'Here's the job description and all the details. They'll fly you over. We'll sort out an apartment for you before you leave, and whatever else you need.'

'How long have I got to decide?' I asked. I was staring at the paper, but had Mum and Dad in my mind's eye. 'I need to talk to my family.'

Emma looked at her desk calendar. 'I have to know by Monday. You'd be leaving early next month.'

• •

'Where have you been?' Libby asked, barely looking up from her computer.

'Had a meeting with Emma.'

'About?'

I handed her the email about the fellowship.

She screamed with delight. 'You're going to New York? Oh my god, I am so jealous.'

She jumped up and grabbed me with both hands. 'Take me with you.' Libby was even more excited than Emma.

'I haven't said I'm going yet. I have to think about it.' I wriggled out of her grasp and slumped down into my chair. 'What about my family? What about Denise? What about my work here? I'll be letting too many people down.'

Libby plonked herself on the corner of my desk. 'You won't be letting *anyone* down – unless you don't go, and then you'll be letting us *all* down, including yourself.'

'What about our program here?'

'Emma wouldn't have suggested it if she thought it would jeopardise our program.'

'What about Denise, then?'

'You're Denise's flatmate, not her girlfriend, unless you've become one of those Canberra statistics and just haven't told me.'

'What statistics?'

'Canberra has more same-sex female couples than any other state or territory.' She poked me in the arm. 'Haven't changed teams since Adam, have you?'

'Oh, you're hilarious. What about Mum and Dad then? Dad didn't even want me to go to Sydney to study. You can imagine how he'll flip at the thought of me going to New York.'

'Lauren, you're thirty years old. You're not Daddy's little girl anymore. And I'm sure Mum Jules will be thrilled you're going to New York, what with all that shopping.'

I was my mother's daughter when it came to shopping – no sale went unnoticed and we both knew the layout of every shopping centre in Canberra – and Libby knew it.

'Maybe you're right.'

Libby smiled knowingly, then went back to her desk.

I tried to look at the emails that had come in while I was with Emma, but I couldn't concentrate.

'I don't get it,' Libby went on. 'Don't you want to go to New York? Are you mad? Didn't you watch *Sex and the City*? The place is crawling with men and bars and good fun.'

I didn't look up. 'I'm not interested in men right now, and you know it. Adam Fuller is the only man I have ever loved, and that's not going to change overnight just because we've broken up.'

'Okay then, look at it this way. Mr Fullofhimself has exacerbated your insomnia by being a jerk. As New York's the city that never sleeps, at least you'll have something to do late at night other than check his MySpace page.'

Mr Fullofhimself was Libby's name for Adam. She never did like him.

I couldn't think straight. So even though it was only lunchtime, I switched off my computer and picked up my bag. 'I've only got until Monday to decide. I need to go see Mum and Dad.'

I headed back to the flat to grab some clothes. Denise was in bed sick, so as I rummaged through the ironing basket for jeans and a jumper I filled her in on everything.

'That's fantastic!' Denise clapped her hands and smiled

like Emma and Libby, but she could see that I wasn't as thrilled. 'Isn't it?'

'It's a fantastic *idea*, but right now I'm more confused than excited.'

'You know, Lauren,' Denise said in between sniffles, 'New York might be the best thing for you right now, not only on a professional level, but personally as well.'

It was the first time she'd made any remote reference to Adam without prompting. She'd been avoiding the subject for a couple of weeks now, ever since he made media headlines.

• •

I drove to Goulburn listening to Kasey Chambers singing 'Am I Not Pretty Enough' and wondering if that was the reason Adam didn't want to be with me full-time, in public. I didn't look like any of the girls on his MySpace page: most of them were blonde, matchstick-thin and had fake boobs. I would never be or have any of those things.

As I drove around what used to be Lake George, it looked like climate change had dried up all the water between Canberra and Goulburn. I felt like I had cried enough tears in weeks gone by to replenish the whole region.

When I reached Mum and Dad's I fixed my smudged mascara and face before I went inside.

'Oh, your father and I have watched all the old movies set in New York, haven't we, Graham. I loved *An Affair to Remember* and *Breakfast at Tiffany's*. It looks like a wonderful city.' We were all sitting round the kitchen table while Mum poured the tea. 'I always wanted to go to America, but your father wouldn't even discuss it, and we could never afford it, anyway. And here you are having someone else want to fly you there and give you a great job with the American Indians. How wonderful. Isn't it wonderful, Gray? Max?'

My brother Max went to speak but didn't have a chance – Dad was already hyperventilating trying to get his words out. 'What are you talking about, woman? Romantic movies? What about *The Godfather* and *Goodfellas* and . . .' He put his cup down. 'And what about all those crime shows we watch on television? Most of them are set in New York!'

He turned to me. 'Don't you watch the news? They shoot each other in the street in America. They fly planes into buildings in New York. They never turn the lights off in that city. Waste of bloody electricity, if you ask me.'

'Come on, Gray, don't be like that.' Mum patted Dad's hand – she was always worrying about his blood pressure. 'Be happy for Lauren going to the Big Apple.'

'Big bloody Apple, my arse. We've got Big Apples here, at Batlow, and there's one somewhere in Tassie and another one in Queensland, so I don't know why she'd want to go to some bloody big-noting-apple in America.'

'Gray, c'mon love, you're being silly. America has everything bigger and better than we have.'

'Bigger? Better? I'm sure the Yanks don't have a Big Banana, or a Big Avocado, and you can bet your bottom dollar they ain't got a Big Mango or a Big Pineapple!'

'And I bet they don't have a Big Poo like Kiama, either,' Max threw in, which even made Mum giggle.

Once Dad caught his breath he started again. 'Oh, and they wouldn't have a Big Prawn, would they? They'd have a bloody shrimp, which doesn't even sound big.' Dad waved his arms in the air erratically with frustration.

Max was laughing hard and even I had to chuckle at Dad being so seriously irrational. As I was Dad's favourite I usually took his side, but this time he was just too outrageous.

'Gray . . . Stop it, please . . .'

Mum looked worried that he was going to completely overheat, but he wouldn't give in. 'There's the Big Mushroom in Canberra, and there's a Big Cow somewhere and a Giant Kangaroo, but ah, no, you women want to go to some Big Fancy Apple in America.'

Dad stood up and took his cup to the sink. 'I'm sorry, love, but the Big Merino has been good enough for our mob for the longest time. No big piece of fruit is going to make me let any daughter of mine go to New York.'

'Gray, Gray, don't be so silly.' Mum went over and put her arms around Dad's belly. It was what she always did to make him calm down. It mostly worked. 'Gray, come on, this is something we should be happy about. Our only daughter gets the kind of opportunity we worked all our lives wishing we could give her. This is what she studied for.'

'I'm with you, Dad. I'd rather the Big Merino, and the Canberra Centre, the Canberra Theatre, and the National Gallery.' Max was mocking Dad – neither of them had ever set foot in the Canberra Theatre or the National Gallery.

'You know I can't think straight when you get that close to me, woman.' Dad tried to wriggle out of Mum's embrace. 'Give a man a chance.'

• •

Dad took us all to the Goulburn Workers Club for dinner. I felt sick the whole time because it was where I had first met Adam, twelve months before, at a charity fundraiser the Canberra Cockatoos were attending. It was love at first sight for me. The minute our eyes locked, I knew straight away we were meant to be together.

But tonight was karaoke night with the family, and Mum was thinking about singing. As she flicked through the song list she said without looking up, 'I think it would be good for you to go, Lauren, to see the world, to meet new people, to move on from Goulburn and Canberra, at least for a little while.'

When we got home, I cornered Max in the kitchen. 'Mum and Dad haven't asked me any *personal* questions.'

'They saw that jerk in the papers,' is all he said, and the conversation ended.

I didn't sleep at all, confusion only adding to my usual insomnia.

I got up early and had breakfast with Dad. 'Come on Dad, let's go to see Rambo.' That's what the locals had always called the Big Merino, but we hadn't been much since it was moved closer to the highway. I had always loved climbing up into Rambo's eyes when I was a kid, and had done it nearly every weekend if I nagged Dad enough to swing by there. Adam and I had been there together, too, late in the afternoon one Sunday when there was no one around. He had wanted to shag in Rambo's eyeballs but I wasn't adventurous enough. What if we'd been caught? It was a small town, and everyone knew everyone.

As I climbed into the eyes alone, Dad waited for me in the carpark. His days of climbing Rambo had ended years ago.

Back at home Dad put my bag in my car and with little sentimentality said: 'Do what you need to do, love. It's just I worry about you. That's my job as a father.'

'I know.' We hugged and I pulled out of the drive and

headed towards Canberra with tears streaming down my face. My heart was breaking for my Dad and I was still pining for Adam. I was a mess.

• •

Welcome to the Manhattan Movie Marathon,' Denise said as I walked in the door and collapsed on the lounge.

Libby was there, drinking coffee and reading the weekend paper.

'What are you on about?'

'Libby and I thought that some fabulous films about New York might help you make up your mind about accepting the offer.'

'And we're not stupid, Lauren, we both know Adam's holding up your decision to go, but we promised each other we wouldn't say anything to you.' Libby sounded annoyed and didn't lift her head from the paper as she spoke.

'But . . .' I became defensive. 'I've halved the number of late-night drive-bys *and* cut back on my text messages *and* now only check his MySpace page twelve times a day *and* only from home. It's just not easy.' My voice started to quiver.

'We know it isn't, Lauren, so . . .' Denise glared at Libby. 'I asked at the video shop for all the movies they had set in New York. I thought it might help you make a decision.'

She handed a couple of DVDs to me and a couple to Libby. 'I didn't think you'd want to see *The Godfather* or *Godzilla*.'

'You were right.'

'Now, we just need to sit back and relax. I've cooked a veggie lasagne, and Libs brought some cakes, so we're set for the night.'

We started with the classic *An Affair to Remember*, first screened in 1957.

'This is one of my Mum's favourite,' I said. 'I think she likes the handsome playboy Nicky Ferrane and she fancies herself as Terry McKay. They meet on a cruise from Europe to New York and have an affair, even though they're both engaged to other people. They decide to meet up at the top of the Empire State Building six months later. It's such a romantic story.'

'Yes, of course stories about people cheating are always romantic, as we know,' Libby said sarcastically. But I didn't bite.

When we got to the part where Nicky and Terry plan their reunion it gave me an idea. I'd go to New York and Adam would meet me at the top of the Empire State Building. It would be far more romantic than shagging in Rambo's eyeballs.

'Can you face another movie tonight?' Denise asked, 'I mean, we haven't even put a dent in the cakes yet.'

'I'm good for another,' I said.

'Me, too,' Libby added.

'I know you love *Breakfast at Tiffany's*, Lauren,' Denise said, putting the DVD into the player.

'It's more that I love Audrey Hepburn's style,' I said. 'I may have mastered accessorising my Target, K-Mart and Sussan numbers to look like a million dollars, but I still dream about wearing Chanel clothes and Cartier jewels.'

'And now you can dream about someone like Paul Varjak moving into your building and becoming fascinated by you – you're just like Holly Golightly – and then he'll sweep you off your feet.'

'As if I'm like Holly Golightly, and as if some hot, sexy writer would be interested in me.' I couldn't even keep a footballer interested lately.

'Why not? You're pretty, sexy and sophisticated,' Denise said firmly.

'And a naïve neurotic, just like Holly.' Libby attempted humour but there was truth in her words.

'Maybe if I went to New York I could learn some style like Audrey,' I said, taking a bite of a Portuguese tart.

'What are you talking about? You've got plenty of style! It's not what you wear but how you wear it. And, tidda, you can buy designers so cheap there. We won't even be able to hang out with you when you come back.' Libby shovelled a profiterole into her mouth.

By midnight I didn't think I could consume any more cakes, or New York couture, culture or courtship.

'I'm ready to call it quits,' I said, yawning.

'I'm done,' Libby said.

'What time should we resume the marathon in the morning then?' Denise asked, picking our coffee mugs up off the floor. 'I'm thinking brunch with *Barefoot in the Park* at ten a.m.'

• •

Next morning the wind howled outside and the sky was grey. We sat in our trackies, drinking homemade mochas and eating almond croissants that Libby had picked up from ArtOBakery.

'This is the perfect Sunday morning. How could I leave this and go to New York? Do they even have mochas in New York?' I asked in all seriousness.

'Jesus, you really *are* a country bumpkin! They'll have a million coffee shops there and so many choices of coffee you won't know yourself,' Libby said in disbelief.

Denise joined in. 'Sorry, Lauren, but Libs is right on this.'

I felt as dumb as I must've looked.

We watched *Barefoot in the Park* and I was intrigued by Corie and Paul Bratter's adventures living in a tiny walk-up brownstone apartment. I wondered what Greenwich Village looked like forty years on.

'I want to run barefoot in Washington Square Park, too!' Libby said when the film was over, reaching for the last almond croissant. '*And* I want to live in a tiny walk-up brownstone apartment in Greenwich Village. *And* I want to go to the Comedy Cellar to see who the newest stand-up comics are.'

'You want a lot,' I said, jokingly.

'Not really. I just want what you're being handed on a plate, Loz. So don't be wasting it.'

We watched the cheesy 1980s hit *Ghostbusters*. I took particular notice of the exorcism scenes in the New York Public Library. 'That's somewhere I'd really like to go – I mean, if I went to New York. The space looks so grand, like a sacred site for the literary. I wonder if they have many books on Aboriginal art in their collection. I would definitely suss that out.'

Libby was leaning awkwardly off the lounge to reach into her bag. 'Now, this wasn't on the bill for this after-noon's viewing, but before we hit movies of the 1990s, I have one more '80s fave for us to watch.' Like a magician she pulled a DVD from her bag of tricks and waved it around in the air so fast I couldn't see what it was. 'Tadaaaaah!'

Denise grabbed it from her. 'Oh God! *Crocodile Dundee*? You can't be serious.'

'Yes, yes, yes . . . I know we've all seen it, but it's a classic. The stereotypical Aussie from the bush who hits the Big Apple. Sounds a little bit like our friend here, don't you think?' Libby giggled as she put the DVD into the machine.

'Excuse me, but I'm nothing like Mick Dundee. I have far better fashion sense, and I may be a country bumpkin, as you keep pointing out, but I'm *sure* I could work out how to use a bidet quicker than he does.' I leaned over and grabbed the bread knife next to the croissants on the coffee table. 'Anyway, I don't have a big knife to keep the baddies away.'

'I could probably rustle up a red thong cozzie to scare away almost anyone, good or bad,' Denise offered.

The last film the girls had chosen to assist my decision making was *Sex and the City*. Libby concluded I was the most conservative so I was Charlotte; she was Carrie, because she had the most pairs of shoes; and as Denise was a party girl but also most likely to settle down first and have kids, she was a mix of Miranda *and* Samantha. The summary done, we watched the film with only a platter of fruit to nibble on, to make up for all the cakes we'd consumed.

The movie made me laugh *and* cry, especially the stood-up-at-the-altar wedding scene, a moment of absolute heartbreak and humiliation for Carrie. Perhaps New York would *not* be the place for Adam and me to reunite. I could feel Carrie's humiliation and wanted to hit Big *and* Adam with more than the wedding bouquet.

'Earth to Loz!' Libby said, clicking her fingers in front of my eyes as she picked up my mug. 'You all right?'

'Yeah, just dreaming.'

'Manhattan Dreaming?'

'Yeah, Manhattan Dreaming.'

'I don't blame you, tidda, it's such a wild thought, you going to the Big Apple.' Libby held out my cup, asking if I wanted another. 'Your dreaming is present and future, not just the past, and the spirits will take care of you over there, too.'

'You sure?'

'Of course. They'll take you over the ocean to another land. But my theory is, we're the First Peoples of the planet, and so we belong everywhere, even Manhattan.'

'Yeah, I know.'

'I think you belong in Manhattan. It looks like the city for dating – the theatres, classy bars and restaurants, even the basketball,' Denise said positively.

'I'm not interested in dating, remember? I'm never going to let another man get close to me. Then I won't end up with a broken heart . . .' I could feel myself losing it again and pulled back.

'You know what they say, the quickest way to get over a man is in the arms of another. And you *have to* get over him. You know it.' Libby could be brutally honest at times, but she was mostly right.

In contrast, Denise always tried to be the good cop, and I was grateful. 'You don't have to fall in love, either, Lauren. Dating is different in New York. You can go to a sporting event or whatever, and it's just called a date.

You don't have to go home with them, but you can if you want. You can even have three dates in a night if you want. A drink, then a show and then maybe a coffee. Three men, three dates, zero commitment. No heartache necessary. I'd move to New York just for that,' she said matter-of-factly.

'You make it sound like all the men in New York are wonderful,' Libby said cynically.

'No, there are cads everywhere, it's just the dating culture in New York is different to here, where, in fact, there is NO dating culture.'

'At least sporting dates in New York would be more interesting than here – they have ice hockey and baseball,' Libby said.

'You think ice hockey is interesting? It's just men with sticks hitting a rubber disc.' I wasn't a fan of any form of hockey.

'It's a puck,' Libby said, disgusted by my lack of knowledge. She knew much more about sports than I did – other than rugby league, of course.

Denise entered the debate. 'Ice hockey? No way, they'd have to be nude to make that interesting. Now baseball – that's a game to watch. Men in tights with big round bums. Yeah, Yankee Stadium – you *have* to go there, Lauren. There'll be plenty of male action.'

I smiled at Denise and to lighten to mood said: 'Mental note to self: tights, round bums, Yankee Stadium.

Got it!' Maybe New York would be the place for me after all.

• •

The movies definitely pricked my interest in the city of New York. If nothing else, it looked like a fun and exciting place. Slowly I was starting to believe that perhaps it was a good idea, that me moving to New York was just the reality check that Adam needed. Or maybe just the threat of me going was what he needed. They (whoever 'they' are) say that distance makes the heart grow fonder, but 'they' also say out of sight, out of mind, and I wasn't going to take the chance either way. It would take more than a few old movies for me to agree to go to New York and leave Adam completely.

With the movie marathon over Libby went home to Ainslie, Denise went to visit her parents, and I went to tell Adam I was going to New York, even though I hadn't really made up my mind. I needed to see his reaction, how he would feel about me moving to the other side of the world. I felt like a child sneaking out of the house when I'd been grounded, because both Denise and Libby would be disappointed in me. But what if losing me perhaps forever – because twelve months could become twenty-four months could become thirty-six months or even more – would make him want to settle down?

I pulled up at his house slowly, creeping along the dark, tree-lined street, trying to see if there were any other cars outside his place aside from his Range Rover. The lights were on in the living room, so I guessed he was probably watching the replay of the match from the day before. He often did that – he said it helped improve his game. Libby reckoned he just liked looking at himself run the length of the field, and loved hearing the commentators rave about him. She was probably right, but who doesn't like to be praised for something they do well?

I took a deep breath and walked to the front door, trying to see through the frosted glass for any movement, particularly any female movement. There was none, so I pressed the doorbell. Adam answered the door, naked and holding a newspaper in front of him. When he realised it was me he opened the door wide, dropped the paper, pulled me into the house and embraced me. He held me tighter than he had ever held me before.

'I've missed you so much, babycakes. It's so good to see you.' He started kissing my neck and running his hands down my body, trying to get me out of my jeans. I wanted to push him away, but I needed to feel his arms around me.

'Wait,' I said reluctantly.

'What is it? Haven't you missed me, too?'

'You know I have.' I closed my eyes and allowed myself the momentary pleasure of him nibbling my ear. Then I prised him off me.

'What is it, babycakes?'

'I didn't come here for this.'

'Why did you come here, then?' He spoke gently.

'I'm moving to New York,' I said. 'Next month. I've got a great job offer. They'll fly me over, help me find a place and I'll be curating my own exhibitions. It's a dream opportunity.'

'Wow.' He rubbed his head. 'This is out of the blue.'

'Not really. If you'd called me sometime you'd know.'

'You broke it off with me, babycakes. You ended it, remember?'

'You were splashed all over the newspapers fornicating with triplets on the Gold Coast,' I yelled. It still infuriated me.

'You can't believe everything you read in the press, babycakes. I told you that already.'

'So, you weren't with triplets?' I held my head as it started to ache.

'No, technically not.'

'What the hell does that mean?'

'There were twins and just another girl who looked a lot like them. That's all.'

I shook my head in disgust and should've walked out, but wanted to give him one *last* chance. 'I'm going to New York and it's the dating capital of the world.' I wanted him to get jealous.

'Is it?' There was no tone of jealousy at all.

'Yes, people go on dates there – to classy bars, and restaurants and the theatre.'

'Classy bars and theatre. Not really my cup of tea, but I'm sure you'll love it.'

My plan wasn't working. 'I just want to be clear about something. You don't mind if I go then, to New York? All the way over there in America? It's like a 25-hour plane ride away. That's a lot further than from Manuka to Bruce.'

'Do I mind? Why would I mind? It's a great opportunity for you. You should go and have a good time. I would if it was me.'

'You would?' I glared at him angrily.

'Of course. It's New York. It's a twenty-four/seven party town.'

'But wouldn't you miss anything here? Or *anyone*?'

'There's nothing in Canberra that I'd miss enough to turn down a trip to New York.'

At that very moment, I hated Adam. And I hated myself for being so stupid.

9

You Can Change Your Life

Toni Jordan

In the two-minute stretch break, the guy sitting next to me says he knows the secret. The secret, he tells me, is positive thinking. He also says that reality is an artificial construct, that positive internal dialogue enhances our heart chakra, that self-esteem stimulates our immune system.

'We create our own world, see?' he says, straightening his toupee. 'We draw good things to us when we release positive energy into the universe. I meditate for fifteen minutes every morning while burning Tibetan incense and waiting for my Chinese herbs to brew. Meditation is great for your chi.'

His toupee is dark brown and slightly limp like old lettuce leaves. The adjusting works; it's no longer lop-sided and doesn't move, not even when he stretches his neck right over to the side. Next we're concentrating on our arms. He stretches his left one up and tilts so that his shoulder leans against mine. I can feel a heavy weight through the cotton of my blouse. His sticky name tag, attached to his sleeveless safari vest, says 'Ralph'. He's drawn a smiley face on it in purple texta.

'Chi?' I say. My shoulder feels like gristle. I don't think it's supposed to stretch this far.

He nods. 'A healthy chi makes endorphins,' he says. 'Like chocolate, but in your brain.'

'Right.' I say. 'Chocolate in your brain.'

I had meant this to sound interested. Or somewhat interested, at least. But as soon as it's out of my mouth I realise it doesn't. It sounds superior. Sarcastic. What Keith would have called my too-cool-for-school voice. *Not everything's a joke, Kylie. Can't you ever be serious?*

Ralph keeps talking. He doesn't seem to notice.

'So. Have you been to one of these seminars before?' Ralph is working hard at the stretching. His toupee is starting to sweat.

'Nope. First time.' We stretch our legs now; hands on hips and right foot out like children doing the hokey-pokey.

He looks at me sideways. He doesn't believe me. 'You must have done some kind of personal development classes before?' he says. '"Become rich and thin using your angel guides"? "The Kabbalah for dummies"? "Positive thinking in a negative world"?'

I shake my head. *Keep an open mind, Kylie.* 'I'm new at this,' I say. 'I'd never even heard of "Embrace your inner winner" until a few days ago.' I smile in an open-minded fashion.

All around us in the huge stadium people of all ages, all sexes, are stretching. Eighty-year-olds and eighteen-year-olds. In the row in front of us are a giggle of school-girls in black tights and flat shoes; to one side are three generations of outdoorsmen in flannelette shirts and Blundstones. It's not right, watching all these strangers stretch. It's like seeing them first thing in the morning when they get out of bed.

Ralph groans as he waddles his hips from side to side. His limbs are utterly wooden and no amount of stretching is going to make a lick of difference. He tries to bend his neck toward his shoulder and only manages to look like a quizzical parrot in a wig.

He taps me on the arm and gestures with one shoulder to a tiny figure, way down on the stage. It's the guru. He's been on that stage, walking and talking and gesturing for four hours straight, and he's still leading the stretches with more vigour than I have ever felt in my entire life.

'He's come all the way from the States. Only arrived this morning,' Ralph says. 'He never gets jet lag because of his vegan gluten-free lactose-free low-acid positive-ion diet. And no caffeine or sugar or alcohol. Ever. He's going to have a long life.'

I nod. The guru might have a long life or he might not. But it's sure going to seem long.

'He does these seminars all around the world,' Ralph says. 'It only takes one weekend, you know.'

'I see. One weekend.'

He extends his hands at the wrists and winces. I must look puzzled, because Ralph explains. 'One weekend to change your life.'

I laugh, then instantly regret it. Ralph looks at me with a pained expression and raises his eyebrows. They nestle in the fringe of his toupee like floating hairy caterpillars.

'Ahem. Sorry. I just meant . . . it must take longer, don't you think? Longer than two days?'

'Absolutely not,' he sniffs. 'Two days is a long time. This seminar can work miracles. One hundred per cent money-back guaranteed.'

'I'm sure it's very helpful but, honestly, one weekend? To change your life? How can you be so sure it works?'

Finally we sit down. I hadn't realised stretching was so exhausting. We begin twirling our ankles.

'Easy,' he says, raising his hairy caterpillars. 'I've done this seminar eight times.'

Now that we're all stretched the house lights dim. The crowd sits, the stadium hushes. Our guru way down on the stage slides into his jacket, takes another slurp from his bottle of water. He's ready to start. 'So how are y'all feeling right now?' he booms into the microphone.

From my seat in the eighty-seventh row I can barely see the stage, much less the overpaid, overhyped guy in the shiny suit. I know what he looks like, though, from the posters hung around the hall. He's an impossibly handsome and tall, clean-cut American. His skin glows. His smile beams. Obviously a result of the no-fun diet. He may be hard to see but I can hear him all right. One of the crappy speakers is suspended from the ceiling right above my head. Every so often it squeals.

'I said, HOW'RE Y'ALL FEELING RIGHT NOW?' screams the guru on the stage.

'We like champignons,' mumbles the crowd. At least that's what it sounds like.

'I CAN'T HEAR YOU!' Our guru cups a hand behind his ear to emphasise, in case there was anyone in the Southern Hemisphere who hadn't heard him.

'Like champignons,' mutters the crowd again, inspecting their shoes. This new-found mushroom fetish is clearly depressing them. They look like they'd rather be anywhere else but here.

The guru puts his head in his hands for a moment, then runs his fingers through his hair in a sorrowful way. 'People, people,' he says. He twists his arms around his body like he needs a massage, like our lack of enthusiasm causes him physical pain. Then he takes off his jacket, straightens his braces for a moment and comes to the front of the stage. 'Let me tell you the secret of life, people,' he says. His voice is dripping with intensity.

The stadium goes silent. The crowd is listening now, as if he were telling us next week's winning lotto numbers. Ralph leans forward in his seat, hands on his knees.

'Life is waiting for you. If you want to be a winner you have to grab it,' says the guru. 'You have to take life by the throat and squeeze it. You can't wait for it to come to you. You have to change your life, be a better person, better in every way. Life is a fight to the death. It's a one-way ticket. Do you want to be a loser? I didn't think so. Now, how're y'all feeling right now?'

'LIKE CHAMPIONS!' yells back the crowd. They are suddenly awake, alert, as if the jaws of loserdom are snapping at their heels.

'And what are champions?'

'LOSERS WITH BETTER SELF-ESTEEM!' The audience is like three thousand trained parrots now, answering in one enthusiastic voice. The teenage girls in the row in front stand up. They're holding hands and swaying. Suddenly the theme from *Rocky* belts out of the speakers, nearly fracturing my eardrums. Da da dah, da da dah. The lights in the stadium drop even lower and multi-coloured spotlights start swinging around like it is a '70s disco. Ralph puts his hand on my shoulder, leans his full weight on me and stands up on his seat. He punches the air, and both the seat and his paunch wobble.

'I'm a champion!' he yells. 'I am!'

Clearly I've got to get out of here. This could be contagious.

I don't care if there's another one and a half days of this seminar to go. I don't care if the ticket was very expensive, and I especially don't care that it was a present from my brother. *Try to take it seriously, Kylie. You seem to think life is one big joke.* Well, this is no joke: if I don't get out of here I'm going to give up my commitment to non-violence and smack one of these psycho-cultist champions, possibly Ralph, in the head. That would really shake up his endorphins.

While Ralph is distracted congratulating himself on being a champion, I grab my handbag from under the chair. With a few 'excuse me's' and treading on the minimum of toes I move to the end of the row. With any luck they'll think I'm overcome by excitement-induced incontinence. In no time I've woven my way down to the front of the stairs. At last I'm in the main aisle and I can see daylight through the doors at the far end. I'm nearly out. My hand reaches up to peel the sticky name tag off my jacket.

'HOLD IT! HOLD EVERYTHING!' bellows the guru. 'Freeze the lights! Cut the music! I need a spotlight in that right-hand aisle! Stop right where you are. I'm talking to you: wavy long red hair, jeans. THAT WOMAN THERE!'

Crap.

I feel a momentary compulsion to run, just bolt for the exit, but ahead I can see two black-skivvied volunteers who look like extras from *The Matrix* standing in front of the doors, arms folded. In an instant the whole room goes black except for a circle of light on the floor in front of me.

I turn around. Now I can't see the stage at all, not with this spotlight in my face. At least it's finally quiet. But not in a good way. I can feel three thousand pairs of eyes staring at me. A gopher comes up beside me, nudges my shoulder and hands me a microphone.

'Just where do you think you're going?' screeches the guru.

'Sorry, sorry,' I manage. The microphone squeaks. I take my phone from the pocket of my jacket and hold it up, as evidence. 'I just got a text message. It's my dog. He's sick.' The silence becomes thicker, like the audience has turned into zombies, like they're not even breathing. 'Although he didn't send the text message, obviously. No thumbs. My next door neighbour. She sent it. She has thumbs.'

It's possible I'm a little intimidated. Perhaps having three thousand dancing champions and one invisible screeching guru staring at me makes me nervous.

Three thousand heads swivel back to the stage.

'Well, well,' says the guru. 'You have a sick dog, eh? An emergency?'

I nod.

The guru continues: 'What's your name?'

The heads swivel back to me, as if we're playing tennis.

I go blank for an embarrassing few seconds and fight the urge to look at my name tag. 'Uh, Kylie. My name is Kylie.'

'I CAN'T HEAR YOU!' shouts the guru.

'KYLIE!' screams the crowd.

'Kylie, dear Kylie. Were you quitting? You can tell me.' The disembodied voice is gentler now. He sounds so kind, so understanding. He really wants me to tell him the truth.

'No,' I lie.

'Are you lying to me, Kylie?'

'No,' I lie again.

'Kylie, do you want me to tell you the secret of life?'

I open my mouth to reply, but he doesn't wait.

'Kylie, do you think I became a multi-millionaire, international best-selling author, blissfully happy husband and father of three, semi-professional triathlete, discoverer of a lost tribe in the Amazon, fluent in twelve languages, volunteer surgeon in war-torn Africa and a world-famous personal growth guru by quitting?'

'NO QUITTING!' shrieks the crowd. Although they're so loud that the sound is kind of muffled, so they might have said 'no spitting'.

'You're right, absolutely right,' I say into the microphone. 'Quitting bad. Very bad.'

The guru sighs, and shakes his head. 'Kylie why did you come here today?' His voice is all concern, like he's that cute surgeon on *ER* and I'm lying on a gurney, bleeding.

I raise my hand to my face and try to block out the spotlight. It doesn't work, so I squint instead. 'You know, it's a funny story. Well, not funny ha ha. My brother, Allan, he really wanted to come. It was his ticket. But he was sent on a last-minute business trip so he gave the ticket to me. So I'm not really supposed to be here. Nothing against you. Nothing against any of you. It's just not my thing.'

The crowd knows it's been insulted. Three thousand heads swivel back to the stage, chins raised and petulant.

'That's what he told you, is it? That's what Allan told you. That he was sent on a "last-minute business trip"?' The guru raises his hands and makes imaginary quote marks with his fingers.

My stomach gives a little flip. My voice becomes a little softer. 'He was sent on a trip.'

'Kylie, can I tell you a little secret? People often say they suddenly can't attend our seminars, Kylie, when what they really want is another person, a person they care about, to come on our journey. I think your brother, Allan, really wants you to make some changes in your life. I think he cares about you very much. That's why he bought you a ticket. That's why he sent you along today. So you can change your life, Kylie.'

'Change your life, Kylie,' hums the crowd.

'My life is just fine, thank you very much,' I hiss back at them. Stupid crowd. What do they know?

'But you mustn't be a very happy person, or Allan wouldn't be so worried about you, would he? Kylie, you know that you're in a loving and supportive environment right now, don't you?'

'Loving and supportive,' oozes the crowd.

'Kylie, I want you to come up on stage,' says the guru. 'Come on. Don't be intimidated. I'm human, you know. I don't live on Mount Olympus. Come and stand right here next to me.'

The crowd erupts in cheers and clapping. 'Go Kylie, go Kylie,' they yell, making little circles with their fists. Some of them are hooting. Coloured lights start spinning and 'Eye of the Tiger' explodes from the speakers. Dah. Da da dah.

This might cause permanent hearing loss.

I feel sick. I should just run for the doors and flatten the Matrix guys, but it's like I'm hypnotised. My legs start to move toward the stage of their own accord. Bloody legs. Traitors.

This might be the longest walk of my life. As I move down the aisle, people lean over and pat me on the back. Some of them chant: 'Kylie Kylie Kylie, oi oi oi.' I'm squeezing the microphone so hard that I've left nail marks in the plastic. If this wasn't so horrifying it'd be funny, although if Keith were here he wouldn't think so. At least I managed to walk down one aisle this year.

Finally I reach the front of the stage. There are stairs, but my legs are shaking so hard I don't know if I can make it up. The guru comes down and offers me his arm, like he's escorting me to the guillotine.

'Awwww . . .' says the crowd.

Up on stage the lights are even brighter, and they're hot. I can barely see the crowd at all. The guru is impossibly tall and thin; I suck in my stomach. He puts his hand on my shoulder and looks deep into my eyes.

'Kylie, may I ask you a personal question?'

Oh boy. Shoot, I nearly say, but I feel a bit like a rabbit in this spotlight and he might take it literally. He doesn't wait for an answer anyway.

'What do you do for a living?'

I hold the microphone close to my face. It squeals again. 'Websites. I design websites.'

He ponders this for a moment, as if it's vital information and he must tread carefully from now on.

'And how old are you, Kylie?'

'Um . . . thirty-two.'

'Kylie, I can see from here that you're an attractive young woman. I'm going to go out on a limb here, Kylie. I'm going to make a guess at why Allan is so worried about you. It's because you haven't found that special someone to share your life with, isn't it? Isn't it, Kylie?'

For a moment I can't speak. My mouth is filled with dust.

'Kylie, I think Allan is worried that you're getting older. He's worried about those lines that are starting to form around your eyes. Your body is showing its years. You're not twenty-one any more, Kylie. You're not getting any younger. Your biological clock is ticking. It's now or never.

Allan is worried you'll never be a mother. He's worried you'll be alone for the rest of your life.'

My hand covers my mouth. Please God don't let me cry, standing here in front of all these people. He can't possibly know how long it's been since Keith and I split up, the week before the wedding. I shouldn't have come. This was an awful mistake.

'Loneliness can be terrible, can't it, Kylie? All those nights at home, watching the TV, with just your cat . . .'

'DOG!' yells the crowd.

'. . . dog for company. Losing your looks, your figure. Looking in the mirror each night, watching each new wrinkle scar your face. That's it, isn't it, Kylie? Allan sent you along today because you don't have a boyfriend.'

'Actually she does have a boyfriend.' There's some movement in the audience, some jostling, the seats of chairs flipping up. About three rows down on the left a man is standing and working his way toward the aisle. He's the one speaking. Before I know it he's climbed up onto the stage from the side instead of coming around the front where the stairs are. Now he's standing beside me in the spotlight. He's a good head taller than me, with tousled brown hair that's too long, and groovy sideburns. His skin is tanned. He has a five o'clock shadow. His nose is a little bent, like it's been broken. He's wearing faded jeans and a black knit with the zip done up. His eyes are brown. They twinkle. He smiles at me, and winks. Then he takes my hand, the one with the microphone in it, and speaks into it. 'I'm Kylie's boyfriend.'

My eyes almost bug out of my head.

The guru puts his hands on his hips. 'Oh really?' All trace of caring is gone from his voice. He sounds like he wants to hit my new boyfriend over the head with a shovel.

'Oh really?' says the crowd.

'Yes, really,' says the boyfriend.

'So, Kylie, out of nowhere, your boyfriend appears? Just like that?' The guru snorts. 'It must be your lucky day.'

Yep, I think. Must remember to buy a lotto ticket on the way home.

'If you are really Kylie's boyfriend, then why weren't you sitting together?' says the guru.

My new boyfriend takes my hand again to hold the microphone up. His fingers are warmer than mine, and strong. They slide between my fingers, his thumb smoothes over my knuckles. He bends his head slightly so as not to pull my arm too high. His eyes have a reckless look to them. 'We arrived separately. I was late. We missed each other outside. Sorry I kept you waiting, darling,' He gives me a wry grin and a dimple appears on his left cheek.

'That's okay, snookums,' I say.

'Ahhhh,' says the crowd.

The guru frowns at the crowd, shushes them with his hands. 'NOT SO FAST! Kylie,' he coos. 'Kylie, I am trying to help you, to show all these good folk here' – he sweeps his arm around toward the audience – 'the life-altering benefits of this seminar. I am trying to use all my world-famous skills, years of experience and Mensa-standard intelligence to solve your problems, but you must be honest with me. You tell me that this is your boyfriend, heh? I notice that your boyfriend is not wearing his name tag. Perhaps you can tell us his name.'

My boyfriend is still smiling at me, still smiling that teasing grin, still holding my hand. I'd like to reach up and . . . what? 'What?'

'Do you actually know his name, Kylie?'

'Ah, his name?' I thread my fingers through my hair, then try to scratch an itch in the middle of my back. 'Don't be ridiculous. Of course I know his name. When you get a boyfriend, his name is one of the first things you find out. It's essential. You see, my name's Kylie, right? So if his name were, say, Danny – well, it just wouldn't work out. Kylie and Danny . . . People would laugh. They'd ask if we sang duets. Rhyming is no good either. If his name were Miles . . . Kyles and Miles . . .'

'Excellent work, Kylie. Terrific.' There is a slow handclap from the guru. Some of the crowd join in. 'So we've established that his name isn't Danny or Miles. But unless you want to stand there all day eliminating names one by one, perhaps you could tell us what his name actually is?'

But before I can speak my boyfriend takes hold of my chin and tilts it up. 'I missed you so much last night, darling,' he says, and then he threads one hand through my hair and he kisses me.

For a moment I'm stunned. I can't react. Then all I can feel is his warm mouth and and and oh I'm lost. The microphone clunks to the floor. The hand that's on my chin cups my jaw, and his other hand circles my waist and pulls me closer so I can feel his thighs through his jeans pressing against my hip. He smells of leather and faintly of pears, of all things. I realise my hands are around his neck, my fingers peeking down the back of his collar. He wears a necklace, a fine chain. As his mouth pulls away from mine, I hear him whisper.

'Ahhhh,' says the crowd.

The guru folds his arms, taps one foot. 'When you're quite finished. What's his name, Kylie?'

I'd like to answer, but it seems I've lost the power of speech. My legs have gone wobbly and I feel a bit dizzy. One of the gophers has picked up the microphone and handed it back to me. When I don't grasp it, he takes my hand and forms my fingers around it. I take a deep breath.

'Well, sometimes I call him unbelievably embarrassing and very forward, but that's just his middle name,' I say, attempting to scowl. He chuckles. 'His first name is Jarrod.'

'Jarrod, eh? And where did you and "Jarrod" meet?' The guru lifts his hands, again makes digital quote marks.

If his front teeth were a little bigger he'd look just like a very handsome American rabbit.

Jarrod slides one hand over my hip, hooks his thumb through my belt loop. 'We met at . . .'

'NO, JARROD,' snarls the guru. 'I want to hear it from Kylie. Kylie, where did you two meet?'

I take a deep breath. I can feel the heat of his hand around my waist, his palm near the small of my back. 'At the track.' I smile, and flutter my eyelids at Jarrod.

'I used to be a jockey,' says Jarrod. 'Then I had a growth spurt. I had to retire. Couldn't fit into the little outfits anymore.' He grins.

I raise my hand and squeeze his dimple. 'I won a pile on a horse he was riding so I bought him a bottle of champagne.'

'Kylie loves jockeys. She has a thing for squeaky little voices, but even now that my voice's dropped, she's stood by me. I often worry that she'll leave me for a male soprano but she's still here. That's just the kind of girl she is, my Kylie.' He pulls me closer, squeezing my breasts against his chest.

'Ahhhh,' says the crowd. The guru gives them an evil look.

'Okay, Jarrod. Let's try a little demonstration for the audience about truth. Let's see if you really are Kylie's boyfriend. What's her favourite perfume? Her favourite movie? When is the anniversary of the day you met?'

The guru is firing his questions, counting them off on his fingers.

I freeze for a moment. Surely the jig is up.

'Your favourite perfume?' Jarrod says. He doesn't look worried. 'It's . . . is it Opium?'

'Chanel,' I say. 'Number 5.'

'And your favourite movie . . . aah . . . I know this . . . *Sleepless in Seattle*?'

I roll my eyes. 'Please. *Dirty Dancing*.'

'You're kidding.' He laughs, like there's something funny about loving *Dirty Dancing*. 'Really? "Nobody puts Baby in the corner"? That's almost a deal breaker right there.'

I poke out my tongue. 'You are rapidly losing boyfriend points, Jarrod.'

His eyes gleam back at me. 'The anniversary of the day we met . . . August 6th? And you were wearing a red dress, suspender belt, stockings and heels.'

'May 27th. And I was wearing a tracksuit and runners.'

'ENOUGH!' The guru yells. 'So, zero from four. Very convincing. You might actually be her boyfriend. Or they might be just lucky guesses. And why have you come along today, "Jarrod"?'

'Just to keep Kylie company. When her brother . . .'

'Allan,' I say.

'. . . when Al gave Kylie that ticket I thought I'd come along.' He curls his hair behind one ear, and looks down at me. His face becomes still for a moment and he looks into my eyes. 'It's hard to meet someone who doesn't take the world too seriously, you know. When you find her, you should look after her.'

The house lights go up, but it takes me a moment to notice.

'Looks like it's time for lunch.' The guru isn't looking at us any more. 'We'll take a thirty-minute break, people. Apples on your right, bottles of water on your left. Remember: caffeine is a drug of dependence. And don't forget your mantras before and after you eat. We'll catch you back here real soon!'

Everyone stands and streams for the exits. The sound system switches off, and the lights. A rush of people come onto the stage; they're carrying a towel, a fresh bottle of water, a folder. The guru waves them away and they take two respectful steps back. Then he looks us up and down. 'You two think you're pretty clever, don't you?' he says. 'Thousands of people in this stadium and they'd all give their right arm to be up on my stage, having my personal attention to solve their problems. And you two treat it like it's one big joke. People like you are only fooling yourselves.' He flounces off behind the curtain, assistants trailing in his wake.

I think we're dismissed. Jarrod and I move to the front of the stage, and he takes my hand down the stairs. He wears an old-fashioned watch; leather band and pale gold face. His nails are neat, trimmed.

The crowd is still filing out. People pat my back, and Jarrod's. I hear one woman say, 'I thought I'd seen him before. He rode the runner-up in the Cup the year before last, I'm sure of it.' Before long the stadium is deserted. It's just him and me.

'I expect you're waiting for me to say thank you,' I say. 'I was doing just fine up there before you showed up.'

'Sure you were. Actually I'm waiting to see if I can walk you out. You're in a hurry, remember? You have a sick dog at home with no thumbs.'

'That's not what's made him sick,' I say. 'He had no thumbs to begin with.'

'I get that. He should consider himself lucky. Horses don't even have toes.'

We walk a little further down the aisle. A slow walk, this.

'You seem to know a lot about horses,' I say. 'Don't tell me I was right and you are a retired jockey.'

He laughs. 'I'm an architect in the city. Trees make me nervous. I've barely even seen a horse.'

He has a nice laugh. The corners of his mouth turn up in a proper semicircle, like a cartoon-character's laugh. His eyes are laughing too.

'Then how do you know they don't have toes?' I say.

'Easy. I've seen their shoes.'

The Matrix guys smile as they open the door for us. Outside the sunlight is unbearably bright. I fish around in my bag for my sunglasses. An older lady walks toward us, hands us each an apple wrapped in a paper napkin. She smiles and rubs my shoulder. 'I can just tell you two are going to make it,' she says, before she scurries off.

This puts a dampener on the conversation.

'Well,' he says. He polishes the apple on the front of his jeans, then takes a bite.

'Well,' I say. 'So why are you here?'

He holds the apple in his mouth for a moment while he takes off his black knit. Underneath is a green paisley collared shirt. He drapes the knit over his shoulders. 'Honestly? I'm not sure. I saw the ad in the paper one Saturday morning while I was sitting in a cafe having breakfast. I looked up and realised I was surrounded by all these people, all reading the doom and gloom in the newspaper, all completely alone.' He puts one hand in his back pocket. 'Everything's fine: work, my friends. I'm going on a surfing holiday in November with some buddies. I've got a lot to look forward to. It's just that . . .'

'What? It's just that what?'

'Do you ever wonder . . . if there's anything more? I mean, is this all there is?' He shrugs. 'So it turns out that this seminar doesn't have the answers. But I don't want to become the kind of person who stops looking for them.'

It's warm for early spring. There are pansies in flower-beds: purples and oranges. Around us, people are sitting where they can, in the shade of the few trees, backs against the buildings, along the edge of the fountain. Some are eating their apples and a few have sandwiches they've brought from home, probably containing gluten. They're sitting in twos and threes, saying their mantras and laughing, exchanging phone numbers and business cards.

I should excuse myself. This is the time to say 'thanks' and 'goodbye'. Shake his hand like a grown-up. I've been kissed before, for heaven's sake.

'Look,' he says. He rubs his hand over his chin. 'I'm not crazy about going back in there, either. How about we go for a coffee?'

I swallow. 'Caffeine is a drug of dependence, you know,' I tell him. 'It's no good for your chi.'

He grins. He rests his forearm on the wall and leans toward me. His face is very close to mine. 'I'll risk it if you will,' he says. 'It's still only Saturday morning. We've got the whole weekend in front of us.'

Over against the gates I can see Ralph. He's deep in conversation with a woman with ribboned braids who's wearing a long floral skirt and a cloche hat. He's saying something important, I can tell: his hands are waving like he's casting spells. She's nodding and grinning. He finds a notebook and pen from the top pocket of his shirt and writes something down as she speaks.

I take off my sunglasses and look back at Jarrod. I lean against the wall, hands behind me. The bricks are deliciously hot from the sun and spring warmth radiates along my arms. The sun's in my eyes, but I don't mind. 'A weekend is a long time,' I say.

10

Letter from a Drunk to a Long Gone Wife

Jack Marx

I thought I'd write you because I've got time and some things to get off my chest. Not that chests and the hearts within might be crushed by truths unspoken – it isn't so, as you and I both know. But it's true that my own heart is broken, and I believe it will only mend if I feel I've made some effort to fix yours, too. You deserve to know what happened back there – all the lies I told, why things ended the way they did on that last, awful night. You probably know my secrets already, clever girl that you are. As I sit here in the apartment we shared (with the bottle we did not), I see that smile on your lip, which you always wore when I lied and you knew, and I pretended I couldn't see. What a funny couple, you and me.

Remember the first night I met you, how I called you a taxi that never came? You might be amused to know the truth: that I never called it. I just wanted to stay with you for a while, on the side of the road, just you and I. Pretty young girls like you are unicorns to old soaks like me. If I could keep you, I thought, just for a time, talk to you, then you'd see I wasn't so bad. It was mischievous, I know – manipulative, perhaps – but it worked. You gave me your number. So, in a way, you and I are forever in debt to my little blizzards of snow.

It was rather the same at our wedding, though for different reasons, which you should know. Remember how the car didn't turn up for us at the end? How we waited and waited, joking with friends, of a conspiracy to keep the old man from getting his hands on the girl he didn't deserve? Remember my rage at the jerk on the phone? I'm afraid it was all for show. The truth is the wedding had bled me dry – the dress, the ring and other things – and by the end I had nothing to spare, the car one last cost I couldn't wear. And that hotel for which we searched and searched, whose name I couldn't recall, in which our wedding suite beckoned – I'm afraid the room was a legend, too, for I'd forgotten to book, so drunk had I been in the weeks before we were wed. I was nervous, you see, about snaring my dream, baiting young meat on a hook. It worked out in the end – you preferred, you said, the romantic charm of a cheap motel. The sight of you in your wedding dress, surrounded by tramps and harlots who cheered you. I will never see anything so beautiful. An angel in hell, I said. It was a title that would come to suit you.

There were those who said I did a mean, selfish thing by marrying you, one so young, and I guess it's true. Did I marry you for your looks, your youth? I suppose I did. Is that so bad? They say looks fade, but nursing homes cackle with proof that minds and memories and moods wither, too. What's best to do? Marry for money? Prestige? The rings? The self-satisfied yawn that companionship brings? Because it's the right thing to do? Or because when you look someone in the eye your insides sink and you don't care why? That's how it was with you.

You never got the honeymoon you deserved – there was an audition, I said, for which I'd been reserved, and so we had to stay. Roles don't come often for men of my years. Your disappointment didn't show. You were always so good that way. I wonder what your face will say when you learn that there was no audition, no role at all for me to read (a laconic policeman in a country town . . . *indeed*!). I just couldn't afford to treat you. We probably could have managed it – just a little weekend somewhere cheap by the sea – but I knew that we'd be alone, we three: you, the promise I'd made, and me. At least in the city I could slip away, down a few and return by the end of the day.

Was there a moment out of all of them when you realised I wasn't going to stop? I don't recall it. Maybe you do. Perhaps it was when I slept in the park, or didn't turn up for the pre-natal class. I remember you on the phone to your mother one night (her hair had turned white), whispering, and I thought I heard you cry. Was that when you discovered you'd been hitched to a squall, married and pregnant to Mrs Muir's ghost, captain of a ship long gone in the broth, who comes and goes, never really there at all?

I don't think you would ever have been so mad had you seen the trouble I went to, in order to hide my drinking from you. I tried everything to disguise it. Sometimes, on my way home, I'd stop in at the corner store, buy a tin of instant coffee and swallow it raw. If I had more money, it was Vegemite, scooped onto a finger with which I'd polish my teeth like a child – a little up the nostrils, too, to mask every breath I exhaled. Knobs of garlic, fists of parsley, Deep Heat (I'd been to the gym, of course), Vicks (coming down with the flu). It's a good thing I was unemployed. It was a full-time job, hiding drinking from you.

It was sad the day you went off to work, good little soldier that you are, your belly beginning to show. You were always true to the future that lay waiting for me, the things that we knew I was meant to do. We were just marking time, we always said, until New York, London – some place where my talents would be understood. I was clearly good, you said; the scripts kept coming, they just weren't much chop. It might interest you to know they were almost always fake, purchased by me from a film fan shop. I chose old movies I was sure you hadn't seen, changing the titles when we'd read a scene: *The Servant* became *Three Fools Rush In*; *Badlands* was *We Gotta Get Outta Here*. You showed up Spacek and blew away Miles.

I couldn't bear to tell you there were no auditions, that I was just drinking beer, out on the tiles, creeping in at night while you slept. The bad news in the morning: another role I didn't get. You were always so heartbroken for me. Don't give up, you'd say. You'll get there. We're fine. I'm making enough to get us by.

There's another thing you should know that might perplex you, I suppose, for it seems so silly now I think back. You'll remember how I missed our anniversaries – all three of them passing without word, or a gift or card from me, just a hand to the brow and an apology, for a memory so slack. The truth is that I never forgot. As if I would – it was the day this old man ceased to be lovelorn. It shines from the calendar more brightly than Christmas, September 11 or the day I was born. It just always seemed that pretending I'd forgotten was preferable to admitting I hadn't gotten you anything, which of course I hadn't the money to do. That last anniversary I nearly did. I had actually put some money away, which I'd hid in the video case for *El Cid*. I took one of your rings to get the size right, went shopping and found a nice, sweet thing, just within my means. I went for a beer to think upon it, got caught up in the drinking machine, found myself at the pawn shop, selling your ring. I returned smelling of Vegemite, without anything. It broke my heart to see you searching, under chairs, under carpets, for the ring your grandmother gave you before she departed. You never stopped, never knew it was hocked. You probably wouldn't be all that shocked.

I did try, you know, at AA, like you said. But, fuck – what an assembly of the living dead! I sat through the meetings and slacked through the prayers, but it was never for me. Had you come inside, just once, after dropping me off, you would have seen. One after another they'd stand in their Lowes windcheaters and high-waisted '80s jeans, and lie about life being so much better, how we were the lucky ones, we enlightened sober, the rest of the world outside in the night, dancing, falling in love, throwing bottles over. Live simply so that others can simply live, they'd say. I'll bet Julius Caesar never thought that way. Or Elvis. Buzz Aldrin . . . anyone else who's been over the moon, or ever in love with a girl like you.

So, I must reveal, I stopped attending, waving goodbye to you out the front of the scout hall, pretending. There was a charming pub around the block, and a handy, late-night corner shop, with lashings of Vegemite in stock.

I have tried more than once to explain to you why I do it. It's more than just sloth, laziness, or greed. It's more complex than that. It's as if there's a creature of some sort inside me, a ravenous troll that I simply must feed. Some say that it's a disease. I wonder why you never caught it from me? You once said that everything you loved disappeared when I drank. A sweet thing to say, had we not been at the bank.

Something strange happened after the baby was born. I found it hard to touch you, as you will recall. I don't know why. I could never make sense of it, and cannot still. I have no explanation at all. It can't be that I found you unattractive, repulsive, or anything of that ilk, for I didn't. Watching you become a mother, a little one growing on your milk, was a spectacular thing to behold. You knew exactly what to do. Overnight, it seemed, you were transformed from girl to woman, young to old.

You kept asking me what had happened to my affection, but you never knew that at nights, while you slept, I would lie in the spare bedroom with photos of you, your flawless poise, your youthful perfection. I studied you under the covers and deep into the hours, loitering over every silken stretch of skin, every unspoiled curve and bend. I fell so deeply into you, the air around us black and meaningless, my breathing the only sound in the sky. More than once, I'm sure, I saw myself in your eye.

So, you see, I was always attracted to you. I often told you I had never looked at another girl, or used one in my mind in a dirty way. It was always true. It is still true today.

At some point – and I know not quite when – I began to panic about other men. It was some time after you snapped back into shape, when our boy was one, when you began going out again, having fun. I became convinced that you were drifting. My drinking seemed to matter less to you. The power inside the house was shifting.

Have you any idea of the lengths to which I went, to catch you out, to find a clue? I hacked your email, went through your purse, checked your dresses for some other man's goo. My drinking got worse. There had to be someone other than me who appealed to someone as pretty as you. I became quite obsessed. Remember that time you came home and told of a creep who had hit on you, wouldn't let you go? He was an actor whom I happened to know. I asked him to try to seduce you, to see if you were the type to concede. He reported to me that you were not. A good thing, he said. There'd have been a stampede.

Another time, I was meant to be out for a night, but hid in the spare room, tucked up in a cupboard and out of sight, listening to you as you spoke on the phone. I was certain I'd hear something I shouldn't. Instead, I heard you speak of me, sweetly, as if the love of your life was me alone. Did you know I was there, clever girl of mine? You did, didn't you? I wish you could tell me your secrets. There had to be someone. You'd say I was just being possessive, over-protective. To this day, I'm convinced you could not have been faithful. It was I who was simply a lousy detective.

I suppose that's why I smacked you that time. I was drunk, of course, but I was jealous more than anything, and afraid, so convinced as I was that you'd strayed. They say there is never an excuse for a man hitting a woman, but that's not strictly true. I can think of a few. Nevertheless, none of them apply to you. I was genuine when I said I'd never do it again. It's a promise I broke, but I meant it back then.

I suppose you were right to call the police. I remember how you cried later, apologised. You didn't know what else to do, you said. You understood that if I'd meant to hurt you I'd have punched not your stomach but your head. And you'll remember that I accepted your expression of sorrow. But I don't think you will ever know how humiliating it was, the sergeant glaring, as if I were scum. She's a fair bit smaller than you, he said, quietly, measurably, wishing me dead. The hate in his eye was something I will always recall.

I suppose I might as well tell you, too: the policewoman wasn't making eyes at me after all.

I have to be honest now with a confession – as I see it, my one marital transgression. You remember the time I came home at dawn, my suit all buckled and no shoes on? I said I'd fallen asleep on the train, looping the city alone, never once hearing as you frantically called, asleep to the air-raid siren on my mobile phone. I have to admit it was all a lie. I had been in someone else's bed. They all used to tell you – and I was one – that I'd be mad to look at other women when I had you at home. But all men are like Attila the Hun – conquer one kingdom and you want to sack them all. In any case, his name was Paul. I have no idea what I was thinking, as I've never been that way inclined, as you know. Just too much drink and too much blow. So now you know.

And then there's that thing that happened to you. That terrible thing. I'm afraid it will shock you to know that he wasn't a stranger – or, at least, not to me – but a wager. A game of cards, the hand of God. I was down in a debt we couldn't afford. He was a bad man. He offered me double: five thousand if I won, which I was sure I would do, and, if not, the key to our apartment, and you. He'd seen you around, had always wanted you, he said. He wasn't supposed to do what he did. Strictly upstairs and no stuff in the basement – that was the rotten arrangement. I guess he just got carried away. I can't blame him. You're beautiful that way.

I remember your confusion when I told you not to call the cops. They'd drag you through the muck, I said, hang out all your things to see. Lawyers would unearth your past and catalogue your lovers (I asked, again, if there were really only three). The case would live online for our little boy, once grown, to read. Best try to just think of it as a burglary, a man taking what he felt he'd need. We could thank God that you didn't take a battering. You blanched when I said it was almost flattering.

I know you'll find it hard to forgive. But just think: five thousand to throw in the wind! The things we could have done! A few different cards and it would have worked out. I've never been lucky, I suppose.

And now we come to the worst of it, the confession I know you will never pardon. It regards your sister, from whom you are estranged on account of me, and a certain spider that dwells in the garden. This is hard, but here goes, one . . . two . . . three: what her little girl said was the truth. Not all of it – she lied somewhat, made it sound more dramatic, but children are like that, sneakier than we'll ever know. It was just a weird moment and, yes, I was drunk, so there you go. She actually did invite it – you know what she's like, flirty little thing. It doesn't excuse me, I know. It was a silly, stupid thing to do. I've never even been the type. I remember, when I sobered up, thinking: imagine going to jail for this crime. It would be a travesty, for it was just one time.

All I give in my defence is the offer – offered once again – that you step inside my shoes, my head. If you'd only look from my point of view you would see it not as something dark and wicked, my bad intentions few. There was no sleaze. It was cute, affectionate – her little tunic, socks up to the knee, the smile that wrinkled her nose and sparkled her eye, like women do when they tease. I did not move until she did, I swear. She was only curious, I know, and she'll hate me when she grows. That's my burden to bear.

But I've never been so touched, you should know, as when you trusted me, stood beside me, against accusations that would send a weaker wife packing. Your loyalty was never lacking. You might say now that you were wrong to have such faith in me. But loyalty is not concerned with such trifles as right or wrong. I'd like to thank you, girl, for being loyal to me so long. I miss my friend. It makes me sadder, still, to think upon what happened in the end.

That last night I got drunk, like I told you I wouldn't, fell asleep and woke in a mood bizarre, our little one gone, the front door ajar. You had always warned me about drinking while he was in my care. What if he slipped out, you'd say, onto the stairs, falling down the stairwell to the marble thirteen floors below? I'd be asleep and I'd never know. Here was the nightmare come to visit at last – I could see his shoe, down there in the dark. I began to cry. Then I heard you coming home, your footsteps on the stairs, rising fast.

A drunk man's decisions are never good, cooked as they are in a haunted head, informed by spooks and goblins who tell him things that make no sense to those outside, or himself once he's climbed from his bed. So it was that awful night, the sound of you closing, my head in the wild. Something told me to save your life, to rescue you from the sad existence of a mother who has lost a child. It was like we used to say about the little one: if something were to happen, a dreadful thing done, at least he had lived a perfectly happy life, never having known the pits and barbs of love and death – life's fickle shears. So it was to be for you. I couldn't stand to see you so morbid and blue, or feel the shame of you having been so right about me all these years.

Did you know what hit you when you stepped inside? I tried to make it fast and hard, a blow that would usher you into the dark with little pain or shock. You dropped. My tears wet the floorboards as I dragged you inside, lay you face-down in the bath. I drank some more while the water ran, filling right up to the top. Then I heard in the pantry a falling mop. I opened the door and there he was, our little one, smiling up in the dark, one shoe on, one shoe off. He must have crept outside and looked but never dared, tossing his shoe down the stairs, toddling back inside while I slept.

I looked up and spat in the face of God, cruel prankster that He is. You used to say it was nihilism – a type of madness – when I said that God had it in for me alone. But what more proof do you need to be shown? I once had it all and then had none, through no fault of my own.

I took the car down to Kissing Point, where you first let me kiss you, and I allowed you, selfishly, knowing all that I do about men like me and girls like you who try to know them. I moved you into the driver's seat, looked at you for a time, soothing myself with a conversation that never occurred, in which a young girl swore she could see the end and wanted to stay, undeterred. And then you let me kiss you, again, and for a moment things were just as when you were sweet and I was desperate – your eyes closed, lips slightly apart, your stillness making me restless and brave, convinced as I was that you merely pitied me, that this was the only chance I'd get. We conceived that first night, I often forget. Then our little one cried in the back, and I remembered.

I took a long drink, climbed over the seat and calmed him, strapping him in with the belt designed to save him, making sure it was tight against his body. He looked up at me with the mad wonder of one who knows nothing of life, and I back at him. Growing up without a mother is just too grim. I kissed his cheek, leaned forward and took off the hand brake, his haunted gaze following me from the vehicle, asking a question I would never shush as I closed the door and began to push. I thought I heard you cry out as the car rolled down toward the lake, but it was only the scream of the wheels under the weight of an old machine that would not be halted until all was silenced in the drink.

I cried all the way home, drank myself to sleep. When the knock woke me in the morning my confusion passed for innocent shock – for a time I couldn't remember a thing, didn't even know I was wed, or to whom, or what time was on the clock. There'd been an accident, the policeman said. You'd crashed into the lake and hit your head, a bottle at your feet, a little boy dead. A drinker, they asked, your wife? I nodded. She'd done battle with booze our whole married life.

I gave a good impression of a man distressed, who could not understand why, or how, he'd lost everything that he loved, because it was true. And they never suspected me of killing you. Because monsters don't come with friends who swear he'd never do anything so sinister – he's a screw-up, they said, but a killer he's not. A drunk and a mess. He loved that girl and boy to death. And so they believed. It was like you always said: if you want to know a man, just look at his friends. You never understood that minds are like galaxies; strangers, until they collide at world's end.

And you never did understand the wretched poetry of a drinker's life – the nonsense made grand, the guilt masquerade, the pathos pumped up to a victory parade, for a man who shouldn't but feels he must. The clumsy percussion of life's rhythm broke, trivialities swollen and good things concussed. A story that sings but never quite fits. It's a life about which I suppose you're not fussed.

But I miss you so much. You are the sky – I escape you one dark pub at a time. There are things to distract me – a song at the bar, a game of darts, an aircraft shadow sliding over houses like a ghost going somewhere fast. Something that reminds me it's good to be alive. Do you see all of this from above? Can you see now that I was once rich with time, and convinced I would never be loved?

At your funeral, I promised you I'd stay sober, and I did for a time, but that time is over. Some keep their promises like rooms for dead children, but mine, they cry out in the night while I sleep, and by morning are lost, the sun rising fresh and sharp in the eye of each new day that must be stopped.

I'm sorry, but I have to go. The night has tinkled and wept into day. Give a kiss to the little one, tell him Daddy's on his way. Stay young for me.

Here's looking at you . . .

About the Authors

ROBERT DREWE

ROBERT DREWE was born in Melbourne and grew up on the Western Australian coast. His novels and short stories and his prize-winning memoir, *The Shark Net*, have been widely translated, won many national and international awards, and been adapted for film, television, radio and theatre around the world. Robert now lives on the New South Wales north coast.

ANITA
HEISS

ANITA HEISS is a member of the Wiradjuri nation, and is an author, poet, satirist and social commentator. Her published works include the novels *Not Meeting Mr Right* and *Avoiding Mr Right*; the historical novel *Who Am I? The Diary of Mary Talence*; the poetry collection *I'm Not Racist, But . . .*; and *Dhuuluu-Yala (To Talk Straight) – Publishing Aboriginal Literature*. In 2004 Anita was named on the *Bulletin*–Microsoft 'Smart 100' list. Her new novel, *Manhattan Dreaming*, will be released in 2010.

TONI
JORDAN

TONI JORDAN has worked as a sales assistant, molecular biologist, quality-control chemist, marketing manager and copywriter. Toni currently teaches creative writing and has written articles for *The Sunday Age*, *The Sun-Herald* and *The Monthly*. Her debut novel, *Addition*, has been published around the world. Toni lives in Melbourne with her husband, Rob.

TOM
KENEALLY

TOM KENEALLY was born in 1935 and his first novel was published in 1964. Since then he has written a considerable number of novels and non-fiction works. His novels include *The Chant of Jimmie Blacksmith*, *Schindler's Ark*, *The Woman of the Inner Sea* and *A River Town*. His latest non-fiction book was *The Commonwealth of Thieves*. His recent novel *The Widow and Her Hero* was shortlisted for the Prime Minister's Award. He has won the Miles Franklin Award, the Booker Prize, the *Los Angeles Times* Prize and the Mondello International Prize and has been made a Literary Lion of the New York Public Library.

KATHY
LETTE

KATHY LETTE first achieved *succès de scandale* as a teenager with the novel *Puberty Blues*. After several years as a newspaper columnist and television sitcom writer in America and Australia, she wrote the internationally bestselling novels *Girls' Night Out*, *The Llama Parlour*, *Foetal Attraction*, *Mad Cows*, *Altar Ego*, *Nip 'n' Tuck*, *Dead Sexy*, *How to Kill Your Husband* and *To Love, Honour and Betray*. Both *Mad Cows* and *Puberty Blues* have been made into motion pictures. In 2004 Kathy was writer in residence at London's Savoy Hotel, and this year receives an honorary doctorate from Southampton University. Her novels have been published in fourteen languages around the world. She lives in London with her husband and two children.

MONICA
MCINERNEY

MONICA MCINERNEY is the bestselling author of *Those Faraday Girls*, *Family Baggage*, *The Alphabet Sisters*, *Spin the Bottle*, *Upside Down Inside Out* and *A Taste for It*, and a short story collection, *All Together Now*, published internationally and in translation. *Those Faraday Girls* was named General Fiction Book of the Year at the 2008 Australian Book Industry Awards. In 2006, Monica was the ambassador for the Books Alive campaign, for which she wrote the novella *Odd One Out*. She currently lives in Dublin with her Irish husband. www.monicamcinerney.com

WILLIAM MCINNES

WILLIAM MCINNES is one of Australia's most popular stage and screen actors, and with the publication of his memoir *A Man's Got to Have a Hobby*, his novel *Cricket Kings*, and his most recent book *That'd be Right*, he has become a much-loved writer too. In 2006, William was named Australian Newcomer of the Year at the Australian Book Industry Awards. The following year *Cricket Kings* was shortlisted in the Australian General Fiction Book of the Year Award. William grew up in Queensland and now lives in Melbourne with writer and director Sarah Watt and their two children.

MELINA MARCHETTA

MELINA MARCHETTA's first novel, *Looking for Alibrandi*, was released in 1992 to critical and popular acclaim. Published in fourteen countries, it swept the pool of literary awards for young adult fiction in 1993, including the coveted Children's Book Council of Australia (CBCA) Book of the Year Award (Older Readers). The novel was followed by her film adaptation of the same title, released in 2000. *Saving Francesca*, her second novel, also won the CBCA Book of the Year Award (Older Readers). It was followed by *On the Jellicoe Road*. Both novels have been published in the US, with *On the Jellicoe Road* winning the 2008 Michael L Printz Medal for Excellence in Young Adult Literature. Her latest novel, the fantasy epic *Finnikin of the Rock*, won the 2008 Aurealis Award for young adult fiction. Melina Marchetta lives in Sydney.

JACK
MARX

JACK MARX is a well-known journalist and writer. In 2006 he won a Walkley Award for his article 'I Was Russell Crowe's Stooge', an account of his relationship with the Oscar winner. He is also the author of three books: *The Damage Done* (co-authored with Warren Fellows), *Sorry – The Wretched Tale of Little Stevie Wright,* and *Australian Tragic*. Jack Marx lives in Sydney.

PETER
TEMPLE

PETER TEMPLE is Australia's most acclaimed crime writer. His most recent novel, *The Broken Shore*, was a huge critical and commercial hit, reaching the long list for the Miles Franklin Award in 2006 and winning the Ned Kelly Award, the Australian Book Industry Award for General Fiction, and the Colin Roderick Award for the best writing about Australia. In 2007 *The Broken Shore* was awarded the UK Crime Writers' Association's Duncan Lawrie Gold Dagger, making Temple the first Australian to win the world's richest and most prestigious crime-writing prize.